INCOMMUNICADO

By

J. P. Mercer
&
Nancy M. Hill

For information address:
BookEnds Press
PO Box 14513
Gainesville, Florida 32604
1-800-881-3208

For distribution information:
StarCrossed Productions
PO Box 357474
Gainesville, Florida 32635-7474

Dedication

I want to dedicate *Incommunicado* to the Angel who sits on
my shoulder and the friendship of two special women. To
my dear best friend, Sue. Friend does not come close to what
you are to me. I give thanks every day that you came into my
life this time around. And to Dee, who's friendship I will
treasure the rest of this lifetime. I admire the woman you are
and all you have accomplished.

J P Mercer

It's for you, Daddy.
You have always had faith in me, loved me unconditionally,
and set the example for me: Just Do Right

N M Hill

Acknowledgements

MY special thanks to Nancy, my talented co-writer; your devotion and long hours are greatly appreciated. We make a great writing team.

Thanks to Aggie and the Professor and all the fans who encouraged the growth of *Incommunicado*.

J P Mercer

Thanks to: Ray Harris, retired border patrol agent, who helped me see the desert long before I felt it; those at Nogales High School, my students as well as Ms. Favella, for all their help with translations; all my friends who have been freely giving of encouragement, advice, moral support, and suggestions; Maria and Raul at Las Trankas Restaurant in Rio Rico, for the inspiration, the ambiance, and the machaca burritos. Nikki and Federico, what would I have done without your friendship and support during my year in Nogales? You are the dear, shining ones of that time.

Thank you, Mel, for opening the door.
May you always see the moon shining brightly upon your seven paths.

My sincerest gratitude to you, *Corvus corax lupus,* my guardian spirit. May the ancient ones always be with you.

N M Hill

Chapter One

Torrid desert heat rose up to assault his senses, stifling every breath, playing tricks with his eyes as shifting heat monkeys danced illusively in the distance. But the image sprawled out in the craggy rocks before him was no heat-induced trick of the mind. He could taste the desert as it crept into his mouth to steal even his spit. The camphor smeared under his nose, while distorting the usual smells, did little to block the sickeningly acrid stench that hovered close in amongst the mesquite.

He paused to look up at one distinguished mesquite whose vast skeletal arms reached downward as if to clownishly mock him: *Look what I have for you, Matt. Here's another one just for you.* Matt Peyson didn't put much credence in portents, but as he stood there, he couldn't dismiss the idea that the haunting silhouette augured ill. He shook his head clear of the abstraction and looked back down the dry alluvial wash, listening, watching. The air, festering with the garish hum of bloated flies, churned his stomach. With a handkerchief over his mouth and nose, he suppressed the gag that threatened to spill the rising bile. His young partner, however, was not so fortunate—Alejandro Ochoa, an expression of nausea blanching his face as he breathed in short, involuntary gasps, clutched at a juniper limb. He felt the slick tree bark, sensed the heat radiating up from the rocks, heard the arrogant caw of a shrub jay passing overhead. Alejandro's cheeks ballooned as his belly revolted.

He heaved his lunch onto the smooth rocks at the juniper's base.

Matt skirted around the perimeter of the scene, allowing the shaken young man time to compose himself. Judging from the novice agent's pallor, he needed it. Walking back to where Alejandro sat, Matt handed him a canteen.

"Might help to rinse your mouth out."

Alejandro sputtered, "Sorry I...I'll get used to it."

Matt studied him silently a moment before answering, "I hope you never get used to this." He took a shallow breath. "How old?"

"Dunno," Alejandro murmured. He paused, wiping his mouth across his sleeve. "Mid twenties maybe," he continued as he nervously ran a hand through his black hair. "Hard to tell in this heat."

"How long?" Matt asked flatly.

"Day. Maybe two. We had to fight back the vultures so it's been long enough for them to get the scent. But the damned coyotes got to her first, Matt." Alejandro felt a tightness constricting his throat. It was like swallowing sand. "God, she's a mess," he said raspily.

Matt nodded in agreement but didn't respond. The two men fell silent, quietly standing against the backdrop of the Arizona horizon. Behind them the sinking sun exposed a peaceful beauty that ironically masked the intrinsic danger of the terrain—low mountains and sloping foothills, bluish in the haze, dangling cloud garlands dyed in reds and purples, the musical whining of the wind in the trees. Twisting tendrils of heat shimmers snaked up from the desert floor to pull the sky down into the rocky land itself, and forced Matt's attention back to the ponderous image lying askew beneath the draping limbs of a palo verde tree. The nauseatingly sordid portrait of death was like a contradictory spot of paint dropped absurdly from the sun's brush. It wouldn't be long before full sunset, and Matt watched the long shadows reach to claim not only the remains of another day but the grotesque scene that stretched out before him on the desert floor.

"Any ideas?" Matt asked with a frown.

"Kinda hard to tell." Alejandro went on, "Like I told you, the coyotes got to her first."

Matt sighed and looked to the sky. The light was still good even though the sun hung precariously low on the horizon. He adjusted his weathered hat and deftly moved closer to study the markings in the dust near the body without disturbing the scene. With attempted hope in his voice, he said softly, "Well, we'll see what Jake can come up with." He paused, then continued tersely, "Alejandro, finish taping off the perimeter. Expand it up the wash, there and there," Matt indicated as he pointed west and north, "maybe another thirty feet or so."

"What about the Federales?"

"Damn the Federales!" Matt barked. "I don't want anybody in here without my authorization. Nobody, *comprende*? Including them, if they show up nosing around down here. And I don't care how shiny their new insignias are gleaming!" His voice was brusque. Alejandro remained silent and set back to work playing out more yellow perimeter tape.

"Jesus, what a smell!" Matt shifted his tone and turned to walk past the sight, past the instinctive gnawing in his gut that had clenched him since he had received the call about the latest discovery of yet another dead illegal...dead hopes, he thought. Each passing day witnessed futile attempts of those fleeing beyond the despair that was Mexico with its devastating sorrow and hopelessness. The lure of *el otro lado*, the other side, was too great not to chance the crossing.

More bodies of desperate illegals trying to cross the Mexican-American border piled up in his mind and in the morgue. But what he saw now was no ordinary border crosser who had misjudged this unforgiving land. No, there was something different here. *The desert doesn't bash in skulls*, Matt's thoughts whispered to him.

When he returned and situated himself at the west end of the body to observe the scene more closely, an unsettling sense of déjà vu hit him as the uneasy feeling he'd had the last few weeks resurfaced. Two other murder cases in the past six months. Well, technically all border deaths were murders, he thought, since the *coyotes* treated these unsuspecting hope-seekers like cattle herded into a slaughterhouse. Money was the only motivation a *coyote* knew. The hopes and dreams of some ignorant desert rat were inconsequential to them. Life held no value. Only the fee to get a body across an invisible political line drawn in the sands counted to a *coyote*, and if that body died, no matter. They still had their money up front, and the world was one less Mexican *pollo*.

Paramount in Matt's mind were the other two cases. For the past few months, he had been unable to put his finger on what tickled at his brain, teased him in its refusal to come clear. Something just didn't add up. Now, as he looked back at the badly decomposed remains of the dismembered body of what surely had once been a beautiful young woman, reality intruded. Matt instinctively knew. His back stiffened. "Son of a bitch...she's not the first." His voice held the faintest trace of panic as he resisted the idea that she'd almost certainly not be the last. "Jesusfuckingchrist," he muttered under his breath. "I've got a goddamned killer here in the desert. As if the heat and the coyotes and the damned illegals aren't enough to contend with, I go and get myself a scorched-brained serial killer."

Matt hiked up the steep grade of the arroyo toward the rim. He stopped abruptly when he neared the crest. A dust cloud rose in the distance, moving fast and getting closer. *Looks like we got company,* he surmised. "Jake, you better find me some answers with this one," he whispered aloud.

Long legs ending in booted feet peeled out of the silver Land Rover. Jake strode around to the back. She had already unloaded her gear and was halfway to the wash as the white forensic van pulled in. A rugged looking salt-and-pepper-haired man in his fifties jumped out of the van's passenger side. He yelled over his shoulder to the driver, "Let's get the equipment unloaded and set up the lights. It'll be dark before long."

The tall, athletic Hispanic woman accompanying him was already handing hairnets and foot covers to the rest of the CSI team. "The coveralls are in the back of the van, Baltazar," she motioned. Tying the strings of her face mask behind her neck, Kalani Trujillo looked toward the gathering of officers at the foot of a large mesquite. A lone figure walked toward the tree's cool azure shadow. As Jake's calm approach narrowed the distance to the grisly offerings hidden down in the wash, Kalani was struck by the irony of the scene she surveyed. She thought, *Just a little over a hundred years ago the Indians around here called this place the Enchanted Land. Not too enchanting now.*

Matt had topped the rim of the arroyo and stepped out onto the desolate landscape that surrounded Walker Canyon just when the van pulled to a stop. His lean and muscular six-foot frame swiftly carried him toward the investigative team as he watched them busily readying for the arduous job. He was intercepted, however, before he made it to them.

"Matt."

"Jake." There was a pause. "Sorry to bring you out so late on a weekend. The light's still good and—"

"Well just be glad," Jake cut in, hazel eyes flashing, "that it was you who called and ended my perfect evening."

A frown tore across Matt's weathered features, and Jake laughed. Regaining his composure, he smirked, "Yeah right, like you were doing something better than poring over all those journals or reading the minutes of the last medical examiner's meeting. Jake, you need to get away from the job more when you are not working."

"Well, I am *away* right now," Jake countered stoically.

Looking Jake squarely in the face, Matt protested, "That's not what I mean, and you know it."

Jake shifted nervously but quickly headed for the wash. Below, two figures solemnly gathered bits and pieces of what the desert chose to surrender.

"What have we got, Matt?" Jake questioned, changing the subject back to the comfort zone of the job.

"Hispanic female, early twenties I would guess," Matt replied. "Dead a day or two...a Border Patrol agent on a routine sweep of Walker Canyon spotted the vultures this morning. Head crushed in, no clothes, but we found her ripped skirt a little way up the wash."

Matt's voice flattened as he locked his blue eyes onto hers.

"Jake, she's partially dismembered...hard to tell if the coyotes did it." Matt took off his hat and wiped his face on his sleeve. He started again, pointing with his sweat-stained hat. "She's about fifty or so feet up the wash there, just barely inside our border. I found truck tracks down the wash about a hundred yards, but the ground's fairly hard up that way. We can't really tell how many crossed there. But further up, over there on the south rim," Matt indicated with a wave of his hat, "we found some good sign. Footprints indicate possibly as many as twenty unloaded. From the looks of the ground where the truck parked, they were losing oil fast. Then the truck drove west before cutting north across the wash. It couldn't have gone too far, and I've got a couple of trackers following the sign. They'll most likely find it burnt out, probably outside Oro Blanco somewhere."

Matt fell silent as he repositioned his hat over sandy brown hair. A few moments elapsed in the silence before he started again, his voice doleful.

"Jake, before you go down there, I need to tell you som—"

"No. Don't say anything. Just let me see her," Jake whispered without taking her eyes off the shadow-makers, the cholla and mesquite and ocotillo that guarded the wash. She removed her wide-brimmed brown hat to run her hands through her sun-blonde hair. After adjusting her hat back in place, she hoisted her gear to her shoulder and headed into the patchwork of shadows.

Matt quickly caught up and steered Jake to the palo verde at the foot of the wash where Alejandro was just finishing up cordoning off the perimeter. Matt stepped inside the area while Jake remained outside the circle. He scrutinized the slender blue-jeaned figure as she agilely circled the outside of the yellow boundary that screamed *stay away, stay away.* Pensively, she peered inward into death, readying herself for the mysteries that would soon reveal themselves to her.

Matt knew Jake would wait outside the circle of death until the anguished soul welcomed her, when death itself spoke to her, beckoning her to come close and discover its secrets. Methodically, she zigzagged outside the taped-off area, glancing furtively down at the sand, peering up to a limb. Finally, she squatted down, pulled on a glove, and retrieved a silvery slip of paper lodged on the needle-like spines of a barrel cactus.

"Matt, are you chewing gum?"

"Nope."

"What about Alejandro?"

"Alejandro, you got any gum?" Matt shouted over his shoulder.

"Sure, boss, want some?"

Jake rose from her heels slowly and approached the line.

"Alejandro, is this the kind you have?" she asked, holding out the offending wrapper as she noted the nervousness in his eyes.

"Sure. Why?"

"Damnit, you've got to be more careful!" she admonished testily.

"Sorry, Jake. It must have fallen out of my pocket."

"Just be more careful," Jake responded and turned back toward the body stowed at the roots of the palo verde. She approached gradually, looking at every inch of ground between her and the body.

"Footprints here." She pointed to an area near a cholla.

Matt nodded. "Yeah, we got 'em."

Then Jake entered the arena of death. She neared the body patiently, carefully maneuvering each step so as not to disturb any evidence. Once she closed the distance and was within three feet of the body, she lingered several minutes without speaking. The silence was inevitable, and both Border Patrol agents knew the drill with Jake. *Stay back and keep quiet.*

Finally, she turned away and sighed. The desert sighed with her as melting shadows surrounded her. She spoke into the gloom.

"Hopefully, I'll get something conclusive once I get her back to the morgue."

As she eased past Matt, she murmured softly, "But I know your question, Matt. Unofficially, I think the answer is yes."

As with any unexplained death, Jake's role as a pathologist was to determine the cause and manner of death, whether accidental, natural, homicide, or undetermined. She paused before she pushed through the double doors that led into the cold, sterile room where the remains of the murdered girl lay. Casting a glance above the transom, her eyes touched the words that hung there: *Hic locus est ubi mors gaudet succurrere vitae.* The Latin credo for pathologists was her faithful reminder that she was entering where death rejoices to teach those who live. Taking a deep, calming breath, she approached the body with solemnity and respect. She had performed more autopsies in her career than she cared to remember, but the job before her was neither a simple pathological examination of a cadaver nor a routine autopsy of a crime victim.

Jake walked around the stainless steel table as she began her initial observations of the body. She merely nodded an acknowledgment of her assistant Kalani's entrance moments later and continued speaking into the microphone.

"The victim is a Latino female, approximately eighteen to twenty. From all appearances, the deceased has been in the desert two to three days. The body is in an advanced state of decomposition and covered with debris." As she spoke, she removed, bagged, and labeled several specimens for later processing while Kalani photographed the body.

"Five superficial lacerations just into the first two layers of skin on her legs, two on the left leg and three on the right running from the heels to midway up her calves, ranging from one and a quarter inches up to six and a half inches in length, would suggest the victim was possibly dragged backwards. All indications are she was alive during severe trauma to her body."

Inspecting the corpse's hands, Jake reached for a pair of tweezers. "Skin fragments beneath the fingernails and bruises on her hands and knuckles are consistent with a victim fighting an attacker," she noted, then paused.

"There is a large bruise on her throat...odd...made by something elongated and narrow. Kalani, what do you see?"

"Hmmm, a restraint of some kind?" she mused, tracing an imprint, an almost *S* configuration within the bruise. "I'll check it with the 3D stereoscopy, get some depth perception. Maybe it will bring out the imprint better."

Jake continued the autopsy organizing in her mind the multiple types of trauma. First, she observed numerous blunt-force injuries, including three skull fractures. One indicated a tremendous amount of force had been applied.

There was notable bruising of the brain, clearly in an outline of a rod-shaped instrument, as well as bleeding in the small vascular ventricles in the brain. The hyoid bone was broken on the left side where more force was exerted, denoting that the killer was left-handed. There was a small bruise on the back of the right shoulder with two small superficial lacerations in the center of it, and the top of the shoulder blade was broken and completely displaced in the area beneath the bruise. There were bruises ranging from one to four inches on the backs of her hands, on the back of her left forearm, and on the insides of the forearms, both of which were broken. They were textbook examples of defensive wounds.

With a disturbed expression, she noted several fractures of the fingers, again consistent with defensive wounds.

"She put up a hell of a fight, didn't she." Jake's voice threatened to expose her façade of cold detachment and professional demeanor.

As the autopsy progressed, Jake and Kalani observed, measured, and photographed the multiple wounds and lacerations. Substantial tearing and bruising of the vaginal area confirmed what Jake had suspected; the victim had been raped. Jake continued her observations as Kalani fingerprinted the three fingers that hadn't been gnawed off by scavengers, but she didn't expect to find any prints on record that would help identify the girl. Still, there was always an outside chance.

Proceeding to open the body, Jake quickly maneuvered the scalpel with deft fingers, making a Y-shaped incision from the shoulders to mid-chest and downward, ending at the pubic region. She then reflected the soft tissue back, revealing the abdominal organs. The second set of trauma came from the stab wounds, she noted. The young woman had been stabbed twice, once below her right breast four inches to the right of the centerline, over the fifth and sixth ribs, perforating the liver. The other stab wound was in her left upper abdomen about two and a half inches below the level of the chest wound.

"These wounds would have been fatal within twenty to thirty minutes at the most. She was probably unconscious from the head wounds by the time she was stabbed."

The third set of trauma was the worst to fathom. Canine teeth marks punctured the remaining fleshy parts of the body, and several bones had been gnawed clean of muscle.

"Note: Victim did not bleed from the stab wounds to the extent that she would have without the head wounds, too little blood in the abdominal cavity. Had she just suffered the stab wounds, she would have had much more abdominal fill, approximately four times that amount."

Jake determined that the young woman had died from a combination of the head injuries and stab wounds. And that she had most probably been dead, judging from the amount of blood surrounding the scene, when the animals got to her.

The overall condition of the body made it difficult to establish a time of death. Examination of the stomach contents yielded very little. More often than not, illegal crossers were allowed almost no food or drink, being detained, sometimes for days, by the unscrupulous *coyotes* who waited for a full load, using the opportunity to extort more money.

Opening the entire abdominal cavity, Jake froze a moment before her moist eyes closed tightly.

"Well, this puts a whole new complexion on the matter," she whispered.

Apprehensively, Kalani moved to her side. "What did you find?"

"Looks like we have another innocent victim here. She was pregnant—appears to be around four to six weeks."

After a moment of silent prayer for the dead fetus, the two women braced their resolve and continued the somber task of recording every detail, no matter how small or seemingly unimportant. The sun had long set and was threatening its presence again when both women straightened up and stretched their aching backs.

"Time to call it a day," Jake said, looking up at the faint daylight coming through the distorted glass of the transom. "Or night."

She peeled her gloves off, and with a gentle compassionate touch, she wiped a lone tear from Kalani's cheek. "We will find the *diablo* who is doing this. I promise."

Kalani's whispered "yes" was barely audible above the hum of glaring, florescent lights.

Jake approached the morning in stages usually, mornings being one of the two times of day she actually favored—dusk being the other, when shadows lengthened to embrace the fleeting memory of day. She loved mornings sitting on the porch with the day's first cup of coffee, watching the sun announce itself over the Santa Rita Mountains. But not today. Having gotten home just after sun-up that morning, she had tossed and turned, her mind never fully succumbing to her body's need for sleep. Opening her eyes, she turned her lithe body restlessly under white sheets of cool Egyptian cotton. Her rapaciousness for the luxury of cotton sheets had been well honed over the years. And while she was not one to put much stock in material items (not that she couldn't afford all the finest possessions) she simply was of a mind that objects fettered a person. The less you had, the less you had to lose, was her thought on the matter. But when it came to sheets, Jake liked what she liked and she never compromised.

As morning swayed over her, she focused her mind just beyond the open windows. A chorus of birds clamored under the scrubby mesquite near the corral, and she listened intently as the overplay of trembling cottonwood tops softened their chattering racket. She heard the sycamore leaves, nearer to the house, rustling in a freshening breeze that sifted the clean sweetness of morning air into her adobe ranch home—along with the dust that kicked up from the desert to invade and coat everything with a fine, sepia powder. She smiled, thinking what effect its presence had had on her mother's incessant need to dust, but Jake needed fresh air more than a dustless house.

A moment later, she shifted toward the window, letting the warmth of the sun ease her further into the day. Crisp sheets enveloped her legs. The sensation jerked her thoughts backward to a time when more than sheets caressed her, back too many years ago when...and she felt the aloneness all over again. She felt it keenly in the other time of day, dusk, when the light of the world dimmed, just before it fell into the chill of an indigo desert night. When she sat out on the spacious wraparound porch in a worn rocker that had belonged to her grandfather, it reached out from the golden red sun and touched her just as it had every day. Then, as now, she felt that tingly emptiness in her stomach. Here in the brisk morning air, she didn't want to look at her life or the loneliness that had wrapped itself into her. She'd always done what her father had drilled into her. She could hear his powerful voice, as clearly now as it had all her life, ricochet past the calm morning sounds to invade her mind: *"Do right, Jake, just do right."*

For Jacquelyn Lee Biscayne, or Jake as she was called since her father never seemed able to forgive her for not being a boy, doing right had seen her through four years of undergraduate work. Graduating *magna cum laude* with a double major in psychology and criminal justice, she had even managed to excel in sports at the same time. Doing right led her to medical school and a five-year residency in anatomic and clinical pathology at Loyola University Medical School in Chicago, where she practically lived in the morgue dissecting cadavers at all hours of the night and morning until she could have done an autopsy blindfolded and probably could have discovered the cause of death just by feel. That was followed by two years of fellowship training in the New Orleans medical examiner's office, where hundreds of homicides per year had honed her skills to the point that she could hold a lung in her hands and guess its weight within a gram. The hard work never left Jake much time for dating or relationships.

She pushed the painful memories away, refusing to linger there this morning, or on the reason that she now lived outside Nogales, Arizona. At thirty-six, work was what she knew...what she lost herself in...what pacified her loneliness. Jake wasn't just good at her job; she was one of the best forensic pathologists the FBI had. Her uncanny insight and ability to see what wasn't obviously there put her at the top of their list of profilers. She was the perfect combination of pathologist, detective, politician, and public relations liaison. As chief of forensics at the FBI's field office based in the U.S. Border Patrol's Tucson sector, she dealt with every faction of the U.S. government, from Border Patrol and Customs to the CIA and Immigration. They were all there in the shadows of Nogales, not wearing "men in black" attire, but behind every pair of eyes was a possible operative for one agency or another. Recently she and her team had been working with the Border Patrol regarding a series of inexplicable border deaths—young Hispanic women, brutally murdered and discarded in the merciless desert.

Jake's thoughts returned to the night before, and the autopsy. She rubbed her nose to free it of the smells that still clung inside her nostrils. It was useless lying in bed any longer. That old restlessness was on her again. It always came when she didn't have all the answers, couldn't find that elusive strand of evidence to pinpoint all the details of a death. She rose, padded across the braided rug that spread across the tiled floor, and headed to brush her teeth and shower. Looking out the window, letting the unique sounds of the desert return her thoughts to the present, she absently brushed her teeth. *I've missed something,* she thought.

"There just has to be something more you can tell me," she said aloud around her toothbrush. Jake settled it in her mind that she had to re-examine the body. All her autopsies were conducted meticulously, but she still felt she had overlooked something. *If there's something more you have to tell me, I'll hear you this time,* she contemplated.

Easing into the shower, Jake turned the spray on and rested her tired body against the cool tile wall. She welcomed the hot water that soothed over tense muscles and smoothed away the edginess that had crept into her as much because of her errant ramblings into the past as by the inconclusive autopsy she had finished only hours before. Just as she stepped onto the tiled floor, the telephone blasted into her solitude. Wrapping a towel around her naked body, she groaned as she glanced at the caller ID. *It's way too early for this.*

"What now?"

"What—don't I even get a how are you, Matt? Or a good morning might be nice. Even a simple hello would do."

"Sorry, you're right, I'm sorry."

It was a long night and a short morning, but I don't have to take it out on him. Jake cleared her throat. "Good morning, Matt, what's up?"

"My guess is you and all night too. It could have waited until morning—"

"Don't even go there, Matt, it's my job."

Matt sighed and launched into what he needed to tell Jake. "We have a suspect in the case. Nogales police picked up a young Mexican guy driving a truck with tires that match the tracks we found a ways up the arroyo from the murder site. Of course, we can't be sure when they were left there, but this guy and truck were seen in the area approximately around the time of the murder. He's not saying anything, I mean nothing, hasn't spoke a word since he was told what he was arrested for. And then he only asked what the girl looked like. Strange, huh?"

"Give me a rundown on him."

Listening intently to Matt's description of the suspect, Jake commented, "That doesn't fit the profile we've been working up."

"Don't know, but what I do know is he'll be held in custody until your preliminary is in and we can run a background check and prints. Guess we'll know for sure when you run the DNA and finish the rest of your report."

Jake sat on the edge of her bed staring at the wall, stress lines evident across her brow. "We're in the process of comparing this evidence with what we have on the other two Jane Does. With the first victim, we might get lucky. I don't hold out much hope with the second one. The evidence was just too tainted. I hate it when I get this feeling there's something we're missing."

Matt scrubbed his face. "Yeah, I know, it has me spooked, too."

Jake jumped up, reaching for a pair of Levi's and a T-shirt. "Okay. I'm on my way, meet me for breakfast, say in about an hour?"

Matt chuckled, "I never could understand how you or your dad could do this kind of work after eating eggs sunny side up. Okay, see ya in an hour then. Oh, and Jake?"

"Yes?"

"We have a meeting with Cara Vittore this morning. She's driving down from Tucson. Just wanted to warn you."

"Wha...Vittore...why?" Jake couldn't believe what she just heard. Her entire body tightened up.

"We got a call bright and early this morning from a higher authority requesting Vittore be given open access to everything we have on this case. If need be, she'll represent the kid."

Jake was thoroughly shaken as she listened.

"The state wants a quick resolution on this case and would prefer it not to be connected with any others and they want it pronto. This case has a lot of people nervous, Jake. Seems like neither side wants this to turn out to be a political hot potato. They're pushing for an arraignment as soon as yesterday."

Jake tried to concentrate on what Matt was saying. "Arraignment! I haven't even finished the damn report! All I have is the preliminary. Oh! Don't tell me!" Her voice turned incredulous and sarcastic. "It's that ass-kissing District Attorney Dan Manning. Must be an election year! And Vittore is defending. Well, good luck to the bastard, he'll need it!"

Matt frowned as he wondered what had Jake in such an uproar. He could almost see the sparks flashing from those hazel eyes.

"Uh...gotta go, meet you at Maria's," Matt said in his low, gravely voice.

Jake sat back down on the side of the bed and felt the hard edge of dread creep into her stomach. *Not Cara Vittore.*

Chapter Two

Cara Cipriano Vittore couldn't remember feeling more exhausted. She leaned her tall frame against the edge of the window, thinking about the case she had won that day, and watched the sweltering sun dip beneath the western horizon from her seventh floor office window in Tucson. She inhaled deeply, sensing the calming effects of the shimmering ball of fire reluctantly surrendering itself to a sky painting of iridescent oranges and purples. Her thoughts drifted easily from the long day's events to how good it would be to sink into her Jacuzzi to soak away the woes and aches from her tired body with a glass of wine. And not just any wine, she mused, but her grandfather's exclusive, soon-to-be-debuted red. Pulled from her contemplation by the shuffling sound behind her, Cara turned and greeted her secretary with a smile.

"Don't you look pleased with yourself," Lara Sandoval laughed.

"Well, yes, I am. When justice prevails, I am most pleased," offered Cara candidly.

"Mr. Torres's family is probably ready to have you declared a saint just about now, I suspect," grinned Lara. "And if you keep winning these *pro bono* cases, you'll work us all to the poor house," she teased. Stepping closer, she said earnestly, "It is a good thing you do, Cara. These people have only you."

Cara laughed nervously. "My dear Lara, a saint I am not, but thank you all the same. Now, do you have the Armenteros motions ready for tomorrow's filing, since I do have to make some money to keep you out of that poorhouse," she said slyly.

"Yes, in fact I just put them on your desk," Lara informed her as she moved toward the door. "Go home, counselor. Relax and celebrate."

"Yes, Mother," Cara droned through her fading smile.

After Lara left, Cara stepped back to the window. Her eyes swept over the distant mountains as she let her mind return to the day's victory. She chuckled at how the other attorneys in the practice always chided her for taking the *pro bono*, thus unwanted, cases, yet were overtly relieved when she did. *Only Lara seems to understand*, she reflected.

Nevertheless, such was Cara's nature to come to the defense of the underdog, paying client or not, in the cases no one else volunteered to take. As a result, her caseload was twice that of the others; she preferred it that way. She had won more decisions than any attorney in the practice. Stepping on toes was not a concern for Cara, and neither was playing favorites or making deals to appease the system. But the long hours she worked, giving each case her maximum effort, took its toll and left no room for socializing or cultivating friends. For her, friends were neither a priority nor a need...being a loner was Cara's way. Her heart would not let it be any other way.

That day's judgment in her client's favor was reason enough to indulge and open her first bottle of Prezioso Rosso, Cara decided. Celebrating a victory over Dan Manning, the state's cutthroat prosecutor, was sweet in itself. But to win Angel Torres's freedom for a crime he did not commit was a reward that almost soothed the longing in her heart for the smell of the ocean and the breathtaking site of rows of grapevines laden with luscious purple, her life's blood. Looking out the window, her gaze met a dry landscape dusted with the ever-changing colors of another spectacular Arizona sunset. The old ache returned. Running her hands through her long, brown hair, she tried to shake off the unease. Her neck was in knots, and her temples were throbbing as the tension increased.

"Enough of this!" she chastised herself aloud and decided a good workout was in order. Taking a long look at the work on her desk, she turned away, pulled her keys from her pocket, and took the stairs to the lower-level garage and her primo yellow two-seater '79 Triumph TR7. Cara loved the feel of its beauty—the sensation of her hand caressing the sleek body and worn, russet leather seats, the intense sensuality of the leather's pungent smell. She thought of her younger brother Stephen...and home and couldn't check the smile or ensuing nostalgia that invaded her guarded soul. Shaking her head slightly, she remembered how Stephen had loved the TR7 as much as she did and how the two of them had worked for months restoring the classic sports car—then how he had tried to manipulate her into giving it to him when it was done.

Little brother, I miss you.

Putting the fine-tuned machine in gear, Cara roared out of the garage, holding the British sports car to a respectable speed. With the top down and the wind blowing in her face, the musty smell of the courtroom soon faded from her nostrils and mind.

After a grueling but satisfying workout, Cara drove up the canyon toward home, with the steady hum of the engine smoothing away the day's tensions. Maurillio Cervantes edged into her thoughts. The old man, her grandfather's right hand of thirty-five years, had taught her as he would any new hire, no special treatment and no favoritism. He had been a hard teacher, but Cara loved him dearly. His sad eyes still haunted her as she reflected upon her last conversation with him. It had been only a week ago, when he'd delivered the "precious red" to her home in the Santa Catalina foothills.

"*Cara mia*, your grandfather misses you, he needs you by his side. He is not so young, Cara. He has been working twice as hard to get the Prezioso to shipping, but so many things have gone wrong, as if *malocchio* watches."

Cara shook her head in amazement at the memory of Maurillio's overwhelming conviction that the wine had been touched by the mythic evil eye.

"He has invested much, *bella mia*. If the Prezioso Rosso does not meet the shipping date, much will be lost."

"Did he send you here, Maurillio? Has he asked for my return?" Cara implored, her brown eyes piercing his.

Lowering his head, Maurillio answered sadly, "No, *bella mia*. He will never, he will never. I know him well, Cara. Even though his heart dies each day since...Stephen...since you went away, he will never swallow his pride and ask you to return." The truth of his words stung her heart still.

Cipriano Winery had been in the family for generations. Traditionally, the *padrone* chose the eldest son to succeed him as head of the family and vineyard when the time came. Early on, however, Cara's potential as a natural-born leader, her charisma and her ability to lead his legacy into the next generation, were apparent to Sebastian Cipriano. At age five, Cara had ridden the fields and tended the grapevines with her grandfather. By fifteen, she knew the Cipriano Winery business as well as he. She could work alongside the best, including her brothers, and had earned the respect of the wine community for her hard work, fairness, and knowledge. She worked as any field hand, and through hard labor, she had earned the privilege to walk beside her grandfather.

As Cara and her brothers grew older, she nobly bore the constant eruptions of their escalating jealousy and resentment as well as their routine attempts to alienate themselves from her...except for Stephen. Cara was sent to the best schools to learn business and law to prepare her for the position she would assume when the elder Cipriano stepped down. The expectations that rested on her shoulders were unquestionable, and her entire life was dictated by tradition, including a marriage to one she did not love.

Sinking into the luxury of the soothing water, Cara poured a small amount of the Prezioso into a crystal wineglass. Holding it up to the light and turning the goblet 360 degrees, she swirled the wine to inspect its clarity and body. Slowly she tilted the glass to her nose and breathed in the bouquet. Finally, she sipped it, allowing it to linger on her palette where she fully captured the intensity of flavors, the mature smoothness with its spicy undertones that finished off with a subtle nuttiness.

The water and wine caressed her, the tensions of the day receded. Memories soon flooded her mind, one upon another. Cara savored again the day when, as a tall and gangly fifteen-year-old, she had been out riding her horse. Her grandfather had come up from the eastern vineyard to meet her. She had reined up and pulled in beside him. They had ambled along, he talking incessantly about the latest graftings he had just received from France, she listening intently to every word. The day had been breezy, warm even. The new grape leaves were just unfurling to shimmer in the glistening morning sunlight. She loved the vineyard, its smells of rich earth and the pliant new leaves mingling together. Cara remembered how taking a deep breath in the vineyard could bring to her the bouquet of the wine hidden within the unborn grapes. She had learned the nuances of tending the vines, caring for the burgeoning tendrils as sun and water pumped life into another harvest awaiting the oaken casks that lay in the mammoth caverns of the wine cellar.

Returning her thoughts to her grandfather, a smile flickered across her face. Cara realized she loved simply listening to the old man's voice. It was as smooth and mellow as his best wine that perfumed the cool cellars. As the wine in her glass dwindled, she remembered the day her grandfather had named his choice and changed her life forever. Breaking with Cipriano tradition, her grandfather had not chosen one of her brothers to take over as *padrone*. She had stood silent and stunned that evening in the aging room as he made his announcement, unable to comprehend his words that were so foreign to her thinking. She, a woman as *padrone*...there wasn't even a word for a female in that position. The conversation still burned in her memory.

"Why me? Better yet, how me? Don't you have to name Paolo as *padrone*? Or even Giancarlo if Paolo declines to take on his responsibilities as eldest?"

"Ah, *bella mia*, *dolce mia*, your brothers, they do not feel the life of the grape flow within their own veins. They are not aware of the beat of the earth underneath their feet as she pumps life up into every vine. Only you, Cara. You feel the very life of the land herself in every grape we harvest. You sense it in the bouquet of each bottling. She entices you. She melts into you as a woman melts into her lover. Your brothers, they do not even comprehend the sensations you revel in when we walk the vineyard together, when we taste the new vintages. They feel the intoxication only of the alcohol, not the sweet sensation of an intoxicating lover swirling within their mouths. But you, *dolce mia*, you allow the vines to take you into their arms and gently offer their delights." A wistful look flickered in the old man's eyes. "I well know the feelings. Therefore, Cara Cipriano Vittore, you are the next Cipriano *padrone*. There is no choice, for the land seems to have laid claim to you as her choice long ago. I merely carry the message for her."

Refracted prisms of color bounced inside the fine crystal and refocused Cara to the present. The water swirled and caressed her long legs and firm, lean body. "Ah, Grandfather, you have created a masterpiece," Cara whispered as she savored the exquisite ruby liquid. For the first time in weeks, Cara felt relaxed...until the phone rang.

Wrapping in a towel, she stepped out of the Jacuzzi to answer it. The rapid voice of Mark Chase, the senior partner in her firm, erupted in her ear.

"Cara, congratulations, baby! You ran circles around Manning. Impressive win today. I know you're tired, but we have a special request, one that I want you to handle personally. This case needs your special touch, a *pro bono* of course. Cara, this one may have all the possibilities of an international fiasco, and you're the expert on international bedlam and law."

"Can you be a little more specific?" Cara shot back, a bit annoyed that her bath and the enjoyment of her grandfather's wine had been interrupted so rudely.

"Yep, Nogales police arrested a twenty-three-year-old Hispanic male for murder, a gruesome murder, Cara...maybe more than one. We don't know if he is an illegal or not yet. He didn't have identification, and the truck he was driving is registered to a Sierra Vista resident. It's not listed as stolen so they're running that lead down now."

Cara groaned with fatigue trying to shake the cobwebs. "We need to make sure he was told without delay that he can seek consulate help, if he is illegal."

"There could be a lot of press on this one, Cara."

"Bad press, I'm assuming?"

"Depends...on you. We've been *asked* to take this case...one of those requests we just can't refuse."

"Oh," Cara snapped back sarcastically. "Where have I heard that before?"

"Hey, be nice. No, I take that back, then I would worry. Okay, you have a meeting scheduled with Matt Peyson and Jacquelyn Biscayne Wednesday at 10:00 in Nogales. That will give you tomorrow to straighten out your case load."

"Really, all that time," Cara retorted. "Jacquelyn Biscayne," she repeated more to herself than to Mark. "Name sounds familiar."

"She's FBI...forensic pathologist with a special border task force in Nogales. As a matter of fact, she was raised in the area and now lives in a little place this side of Nogales called Rio Rico. Can't imagine anybody with her credentials actually wanting to stay in that border hellhole. Anyway, what case details we have so far are on your desk. I want to go over a few things with you before the meet, so be in my office first thing in the morning. Oh, and Cara, don't forget we have a good prospect to fill the slot in corporate law that will be looking us over the end of next week." He cleared his throat and lightened his tone. "We want to put our best foot forward. I expect you to be there with all that irresistible charm of yours."

Obvious irritation colored her voice. "Sure, sure, Mark, flattery will get you...nowhere. You know how much I just love it when you spring for dinner. You're such a cheap SOB. Now let me get some sleep," she yawned and hung up the phone.

A voice spoke up in her head as she drove along the winding ribbon high-desert road toward home. *Trust your instincts.* Jake had reexamined the girl's body, read and re-read notes, tested for trace evidence well into another night. *Trust your instincts.* Funny how the rumbling voice in her head always sounded like her dad's. "What I wouldn't give to have you here with me now, Daddy," she said aloud as she pulled into the driveway of the ranch house. Trudging inside, she glanced at the note pinned to the refrigerator. "Ah, Juanita, I'm too tired to eat tonight."

She switched off the lights and headed for her bedroom, too exhausted to care where her clothes landed as she left a trail of jeans, shirt, bra, and shoes that ended at her bed. Throwing back the Navajo quilt, Jake eased her nude body into the soothing caress of freshly laundered sheets. Yet sleep eluded her in spite of her fatigue, and she lay staring at the ceiling, unable to shake the police artist's composite of the beautiful Hispanic woman from her mind.

The picture haunted her as much as the young woman's actual eyes had, dead eyes floating out of ravaged innocence. It was a gut feeling, but Jake knew there had to be more, something the body had yet to reveal. *But what? What are you trying to tell me?* Finally, Jake succumbed to the day's grueling demands, and she fell into a fitful sleep, only to be awakened by the familiar voice. *Trust your instincts, baby.*

Rolling over to look at the clock, she droned an exasperated growl. *4:30. I might as well get up and read over the autopsy report again,* she thought as she swung her legs off the edge of the bed, grabbed a robe, then reluctantly walked bleary-eyed to the kitchen where she had unceremoniously dumped her briefcase only hours before. After flicking the switch on her coffeepot, Jake retrieved the file and thumbed past the autopsy photos to the report itself. Daylight hovered just outside while she read it carefully line by line, although she had written it herself, in the hope that another review of every detail might lead her mind in the direction of a clue, any clue. Then she pulled the set of photos her team had taken at the crime scene. Meticulously scanning every inch of each photo, she compared them with the notes from her preliminary examination of the body at the scene. After perusing the contents of the file for what must have been the tenth time, Jake was therapeutically caffeinated but no closer to an answer than before.

I'm sure Vittore will have plenty of questions, Jake thought sarcastically as she tightly clenched her jaw. *But I just don't have any answers.* And that realization was like a hard fist in her stomach.

Jake remembered her testimony as an expert witness presenting the DNA evidence for the prosecution. She shuddered, recalling the defense attorney's cross-examination and her ill-fated encounter with the illustrious Cara Vittore. It was another murder case—one no lawyer would willingly touch. But Cara Vittore did. Jake's pretrial review convinced her that the prosecution would get a conviction. Yet Vittore, who had sunk her teeth into that case with a vengeance, had wrangled a mistrial and then managed to convince a second jury that her client was next in line to God himself.

I still think he was guilty, Jake reflected as the impressions of Vittore coalesced into a mental picture of the woman. She felt a shiver run down her spine and grimaced at the fact that the woman could cause such an adverse physical reaction. Her eyes, a cunning predatory brown, were the first trait Jake had noticed that day as she surveyed the scene. Then Vittore's consummate expertise as a litigator of the shrewdest caliber was manifested from her opening statement before the jury to the confrontational thrashing of each witness to the meticulous undermining of the prosecution's crucial body of evidence. She was spectacular to watch, dark hair and eyes—her lean body adroitly posturing in front of the jury like a matador preparing for the kill, mesmerizing her target, daring their defiance, refusing all possible outcomes but victory. Voice and words wove magically to captivate and thus maneuver each juror's mind toward her ultimate objective. And if the power of her voice hadn't completely swayed them, the compelling intensity of those eyes was the final, irresistible gambit.

She was like some kind of Svengali, weaving a spell and taking hostages. They didn't have a chance in hell, thought Jake. This was the tarnished picture Jake conjured of Cara Vittore, an image of a ruthless woman whose presence demanded attention even while her demeanor remained distant, strictly professional, and extraordinarily impersonal. Glancing up from her notes to the clock, Jake muttered, "Damn, I'm late, and I promised to meet Matt before the meeting." After tossing her notes into her briefcase, she hurriedly threw on a pair of jeans, her boots, and a long-sleeved shirt and headed out the door to Maria's Café.

Matt was standing in front of the café talking to Vittore, both so engrossed in conversation that they never noticed Jake's arrival. *Just what I need this early in the morning, Cara Vittore*, Jake grumbled inwardly and slipped through the side door of Maria's Café to forestall the inevitable. This morning, she had the place all to herself. She needed the solitude and quiet before this little soiree commenced.

"Good morning, Jacquelyn," greeted Maria, the owner of the café, noticing the tiredness in Jake's face and eyes. "The usual, *mi belleza?*"

"As much as I would like to order margaritas from now until the end of the day, yes, Maria, please, the usual. Oh, with a double dose of powered sugar."

Maria set the white-coated sopaipillas in front of Jake and asked, "Keep an eye on the place, Jake, will you? If you need more coffee, you know where to get it. I need to get a few things from the stock room."

Jake sat nursing a cup of extra-strong black coffee when a shadow fell over her. She turned toward it and almost dropped her cup as she came face to face with the woman she had hoped never to see again. Vittore looked at her absentmindedly and laughed at the specks of white powered sugar dotting Jake's nose and face.

"I need some coffee urgently. Is anyone here?" Cara impatiently asked as she sat at the counter beside Jake. "And you need to wash your face," she added, a raised eyebrow mocking Jake while she leveled her eyes on the blonde. A faint smirk threatened the corner of Cara's mouth.

"Excuse me, but rude is as rude does. Does everyone snap to attention at your beck and call?" Jake angrily retorted as she piercingly focused on the same dark eyes that had tormented her memory for two years.

Jake reached up to wipe her face, but her hand stopped suddenly. Startled at her realization that she'd been staring, she knew she had to do something quickly before she hastily said anything more. Irritated, she hopped up and went around the counter to the coffee urns. The same sense of dread as she'd felt the last time she suffered under the gaze of this woman followed her.

"How strong do you want it?" she asked, trying to scrape some of the sugar off her fingers and face.

"I don't know. How strong have you got it?"

Jake looked down at her own cup, still firmly clutched in one hand. "Well, we do have this very mean blend of French Roast that is guaranteed to keep you sleepless for...oh, at least the next forty-eight hours," she suggested.

"Mmm..." Cara tapped one finger on the heavy porcelain cup in front of her, contemplating the brashness of the other woman. *Oh what the hell, I'm too tired to spar this morning.* "I could definitely do with some of that."

Just as Jake was trying to pour the coffee without burning herself or the self-righteous woman across the counter from her, the café door swung open and Matt sauntered in with a grin plastered on his face. "And this would be your day job now?" he joked.

Before Jake could respond, Matt kept up his line of teasing. "Well now, since you're in charge here, do you think you could rustle me up some grub?" he said with affection and mischief in his voice. His eyes hungrily roamed over Jake from the tips of her boots to the smudges of powered sugar on her face while he turned a cup over. "And I sure could use a shot of that coffee 'bout now too, Jake."

"Matt, you'll be wearing this coffee if you aren't careful," Jake growled with feigned indignation.

Cara watched the exchange with a detached interest, unaware that the woman who had taken an obvious dislike to her since she came into the café was Jacquelyn Biscayne, the forensic expert whose testimony she had quashed two years ago. With her eyes still on Jake and the pot of hot coffee, she mused, *she wouldn't, would she?*

Directing her attention away from Matt to the scrutinizing dark woman, Jake offered, "Do you need warmed up a bit, Counselor?"

Counselor? Do I know this woman?

Jake groaned inwardly as Cara's questioning brown eyes pinned her. She felt the heat creeping up her neck when she suddenly realized this woman didn't recognize her, and it fueled her annoyance even more.

Continuing to stare unflinchingly into Jake's hazel eyes, Cara didn't hesitate with her reply. "Yes, please do."

Jake's hands started to tremble slightly, but she did manage to get most of the coffee in the woman's cup just as Matt rounded the counter behind her.

"Maria!" he shouted. "Where is my favorite cook this morning? Maria! Get your pretty self out here. I'm starving!"

Just then, Maria came through the kitchen door with her arms full of paper napkins to refill the containers on the counter and tables. Hastily, she dropped the bundles onto the counter, straightened her crisp white apron, and poked her finger into his chest, backing him away with each jab.

"Let's get one thing straight, Matt Peyson, I am your only cook, *mi hijo*. All you can do is burn the water and scorch the air when it comes to cooking. You need to find a good woman to settle down with. Make me a *nieta* before her *abuelita* is too old to spoil her."

Matt cautioned a glance at Jake. Her eyes were quick to avoid his, and she retreated to the other side of the counter.

"I'm working on it, Mama, I'm working on it." Matt muttered, sidetracked by Jake's response to Maria's prodding.

The woman's fierce expression changed into hearty laughter as she attempted to lessen the tension her remarks about grandchildren had caused in Jake.

"Still chasing my help around the counter? I swear I don't know which one, you or Sandro, had more boyfriends and husbands tearing my place up! Speaking of Sandro, where has that silver-tongued devil been hiding? I've not seen my *sobrino* for a while."

"He had a couple of new horses he was breaking in, so I imagine that's been keeping him tied up."

Aware of her son's unsettled appearance disguised behind his façade of a smile, Maria touched Matt's arm gently. "Go sit down with Jacquelyn. I'll make your breakfast."

Then more loudly, she chastised, "And please take your hat off, Matt. A gentleman nev—"

"Never wears his hat at the table," he recited, grabbing Maria around the waist and kissing her cheek, while throwing his hat on the counter, "Yes, Mama, but please tell Miss Biscayne here that I am a preferred customer, and I get hot coffee, too," he teased.

Cara had remained silent throughout the entire interplay behind the counter. She was well aware of the insinuating undertones in Matt's teasing and very conscious of how uncomfortable it made the blonde.

She smiled and warmed into a chuckle at Matt's affection for the woman who was obviously not just the proprietor of the café and how Matt had unwittingly revealed her mistake at assuming the irritating jean-clad woman was the waitress.

So this is the FP I have the meeting with. Jacquelyn Biscayne, well, well...most interesting. Ah yes, I remember her now. Two years ago. I seem to recall she looked at me like she hated my guts...like I was a shyster who was smooth talking a jury into letting a murderer go free. Her testimony was most impressive...if anything, it alone could have buried my client, and would have if I hadn't gotten the mistrial and most of the forensic evidence thrown out on a procedural technicality. If I remember correctly, actually due to an error she made. Giving Jake a thorough once over, she wondered, *Hmm, how I could have forgotten her or that ill temper!*

Directing her attention to the new customer in her café, Maria apologized. "You'll forgive him, miss. He's always like this until I get him fed. Then he's just like the rest of them—rude, ungrateful, thankless, and ill mannered. Not like Jake here at all. Oh, and Jake, thanks for watching the front and getting coffee."

"I'm Maria Peyson, pleased to meet you, Miss...?"

"Vittore, Cara Vittore," taking the offered hand.

"Has Jake taken care of you, Miss Vittore?"

"Please, call me Cara. And yes," glancing back to Jake, "so far."

Jake forgot her nervousness as her hazel eyes turned to glacial green remembering who this woman was sitting across from her, the cunning, cold-as-ice attorney who had methodically neutralized weeks of work gathering and analyzing evidence.

The faces of the murdered couple's family had kept Jake awake many a night. They had felt betrayed by a justice system that protected the guilty, abandoning the innocent victims on a mere technicality. *Well, not this time, Vittore!* Jake steadied her emotions, drained the last of her coffee, and determinedly walked toward the door. Her voice trailed after her in a tone that left no doubt in anyone's mind that she meant business.

"I'll see you both in my office when you're through socializing."

Jake was gone, leaving three stunned observers who had no idea what the hell had just happened in the now silent café. And Jake had no idea that her outlook on Cara Vittore would that day be forever changed.

Chapter Three

Jake stormed into her office, chiding herself ruthlessly for losing control in the café. She strode over to the open window and stared out. A light breeze billowed her white cotton shirt and ruffled her hair. "Impossible, this is never going to work," she hissed, then wheeled back to her desk where she impetuously started sorting through the papers, sightlessly glancing over nondescript folders and files. She was oblivious to Kalani's silent approach.

"You're upset about something. Do you want to tell me about it?" Kalani asked quietly, observing the slight tightening to Jake's entire posture. She could see her hands clenching and unclenching with each stack of papers she aimlessly shuffled around. Storm-clouded hazel eyes flashed a silent warning at the sudden intrusion, then refocused on the superfluous array of papers in front of her.

Unfazed by the attitude, Kalani demanded full attention. "Don't."

"Don't what, Kalani?"

"Keep shutting yourself off from people. Jake, I've known you too long, and I can read you too well. What's wrong?"

The noisy shuffle stopped. Jake swiveled in her chair to face Kalani. "The tissue samples, are you finished with them?"

Kalani accepted her need for space. Which was not to say she wasn't still worried. She merely gave a low laugh accompanied by a tilt of her head. "Okay, I'll give you this one, although you need lessons in changing the subject. As for the samples, yes, I'm finished. Most were contaminated, but," a tenacious look of self-satisfaction suffused Kalani's face as she handed Jake the report, "here's the last one I ran."

Jake eagerly read the results, her lips curling slightly into a half smile. "Good! Good! Let's get the order out for a tissue sample from the suspect and compare them," Jake directed, not looking up from her reading. "Everything by the book, K. Follow protocol to the letter."

I won't give her another chance to manipulate evidence in her favor, not this time. Although...I don't think this kid is our killer. Only a brutal, crazed sadist could carry out such butchery. Who could stomach doing this? My guess, someone who has done this before and will do it again.

"One step ahead of you, Jake. Already got the order early this morning."

Jake nodded, pleased that Kalani had handled the matter with her usual blend of logic and precision.

Cara moved over to the large plate-glass café window to finish her coffee. Nogales, like so many other border towns, was a flurry of activity. Though it was only eight o'clock in the morning, the streets leading to and from the border crossing were packed with an eclectic mix of curious tourists, residents, shoppers, and Border Patrol agents. The weather was oppressively warm already, and the tinny rhythm of Latin music could be heard blaring through the open windows of passing cars. Paying no attention when Matt's cell phone rang, she sipped her coffee, purposefully trying to prepare herself for the imminent collision with Jake. She shifted her position slightly to get a better view of the street, leaving Matt's light-hearted burr in the background.

"Sandro, speak of the devil, we were just talking about you," Matt laughed.

"And how is my beautiful aunt?"

"As ornery and beautiful as ever, *mi amigo*. What's up with you today?"

"Ugly business, this murder in the desert, Matt."

"Murders, Sandro, murders. We suspect there is a correlation between the deaths of two other Jane Does and the one we recovered this week. Work of a sick bastard. Hey, where are you anyway?"

"In your office, *compadre*. Can we meet?"

"Come on over to Mama's, coffee's on. I'm here with the attorney for the kid we picked up."

"A mouthpiece in a suit, huh. Who is he, Matt?"

"She. It's Cara Vittore out of Tucson. She's here for a briefing on what we have so far."

"What!" Sandro couldn't suppress his surprise. "Isn't that the fucking prosecutor's job, Matt, to give her the evidence?"

"As a rule, yes, but this was cleared through District Attorney Manning's office. He didn't like it either, but his office was under pressure to make an exception in this case."

Looking apologetically toward Cara, Matt shrugged. "Now get your carcass over here and say hello to the best cook this side of the border, she's been missing your smooth-talking ways."

With that, Matt flipped his phone closed.

The last part of his conversation tugged Cara out of her thoughts. As she looked pointedly at him, her face was a study of expressionless professionalism.

"I'll go ahead to the briefing. Oh, I would like to see the crime scene today, too, before I see my client. If that's all right?" Cara said as she moved toward the door, her calm voice never betraying her underlying tension.

Matt stared at Cara a long moment, his thoughts obviously elsewhere. "Sure thing. Tell Jake I'll be along shortly. If you're in a hurry, ask her to drive you on out."

When he'd watched her disappear around the corner, he rubbed a hand through his hair and remembered that Jake was pissed beyond belief. He sighed sympathetically. *Good luck, Cara...I hope you have a clue how to deal with her.* His relationship with Jake was predictable: one step forward, three steps back. Whenever he got too close, she pushed him away.

"Well, hasn't this been an interesting morning," Maria quipped incredulously from behind the counter.

"My sentiments exactly, Mama."

Cara paid no attention to the cacophony of sounds that surrounded her as she strode resolutely to Jake's office. She walked briskly down the street, a pair of dark shades concealing the determination in her eyes. Her mood deflated exponentially the closer she got. By the time she reached the door, she had marshaled her features into a calm mask that did not betray the harrowing annoyance she felt. That little something in the back of her mind that always flashed a warning was a glaring neon red just now. Even though she knew this meeting was not going to be an amicable one if the animosity in the café was any indication, she hoped that she would be able to maintain her composure for the duration.

What is it about her that just gets me going? I suppose it doesn't matter—I'm just here long enough to get what's needed for the case, and I'll be damned if I'll let this hot-tempered doctor put me off.

Distracted by the incident in the café, Jake let out a vexed sigh and reached up to rub her temples. She had been engrossed in her work for the past few days, sitting for hours at a time at her computer or desk poring over photos and evidence sheets, and that combined with the lack of physical activity and sleep was making her antsy. Worse, it was causing her mind to wander. She had hated Cara on sight this morning, a feeling that only intensified as the day wore on. She hated her arrogantly nonchalant voice, her obvious cleverness in the fine art of manipulation. No! It would be a cold day in hell before she let this woman get the best of her again. Then in a flash of truthfulness, Jake suddenly could see how the situation with Vittore would be detrimental, possibly even an obstruction to her impartiality in the case. Being completely honest with herself, she finally admitted that the root of this conflict was fear. Fear that another killer would go free. Fear that Vittore would humiliate her again. And this morning, even fear that she could not deal with her relationship with Matt.

It's not about you, Jake. Just let it go and get on with the job.

At that moment, she sensed Cara standing in the doorway. She'd been dreading this conversation from the moment Matt had told her Vittore was on the case. Without looking up, Jake indicated with a hand that Cara should sit.

Cara regarded Jake for a moment, wishing she would cease with the attitude. *Well if she thinks I have time to stand or sit and wait like a chastised child, she's wrong!* Agitated further by the rudeness, Cara stood her ground.

When no response was forthcoming, Jake raised her eyes to Cara's and was promptly hit with the attorney's resolute, no-nonsense voice.

"Let's get this over with. If you have something to say, say it. I don't want to trip over this every time we have to be in the same room, or for that fact in the same town!"

Two years of nursing the resentment came to a full head of steam.

"You're absolutely right, let's," Jake hurled as she rose, leaned across her desk into the dark, menacing eyes, and fixed Cara with a cold, direct stare. Implicit in the piercing gaze of both women was all the anger and frustration each was attempting to keep in check. Repressing a desire to inflict immediate and serious bodily harm, she warned Cara. "But keep in mind, you're not in a courtroom now, and I won't go running from the legendary Cara Vittore this time."

Cara allowed herself a small smile at the thought of Jake running scared. *One of the FBI's most formidable pathologists and profilers devastated by her courtroom fiasco. Who'd have thought?*

"I didn't know you ran the last time," Cara retorted smugly.

Jake stared at her, watching the corners of Cara's mouth lift. "No, you wouldn't! To put it bluntly, you're too self-absorbed," she flipped back.

"Get this straight, lady, I was doing my job. I believed then, and I still believe it now—my client was innocent. Let's put this where it belongs. If you hadn't screwed up, I wouldn't have gotten the evidence thrown out, now would I? So if he was guilty, you're the one who set him free. What? Just easier on your conscience to blame me?"

Jake was livid. "You humiliated me on the stand without mercy, you questioned my competency and got months of goddamn good work thrown out, so don't give me your goddamned righteous indignation!" Jake yelled, all patience gone, slamming her hand down on the desk.

"You seem to have survived the incident without too many scars," Cara sneered in a low, impatient voice, leaning across her side of the desk.

Irrational defiance spilled over the hostile space between them, neither woman giving an inch. Kalani, who had witnessed the confrontation and felt an acute unease pool in her stomach, decided Custer's Last Stand was being re-enacted and that it might get bloody at any moment.

"Time—time out ladies. I'm sorry to interrupt your fun here, but...how about a truce. This is a no-win situation."

Through eyes narrowed to minuscule slits, Jake stared into a whirlpool that was pulling everything into its depths. She felt the air in her lungs being sucked out by the intense inferno that was Cara Vittore. The vehemence of the moment was palpable. Jake's grip on the desk turned her knuckles white. Her head was spinning as she looked into an angry vortex of molten brown. The same powerlessness of two years ago on a witness stand before this woman threatened to overwhelm her. Intense and hypnotic energy radiated from Cara. She could smell it, feel it scorch her psyche just as it had the last time.

Cara was seething, mostly at herself for allowing this woman to get beneath her impenetrable outer shell, her safe haven over the years. The only time she allowed her emotions into play was when she combined them with her legal ingenuity to represent the unfortunate...the guilty until proven innocent...those who had neither means nor money to navigate the labyrinthine justice system. She had always been nothing but strong and unwavering, always in complete control. Never had she allowed such unguarded emotion to spill forth. This woman, however, incensed her beyond reason, which infuriated her even more.

The three women stood in silence, Jake and Cara still glowering at each other. Both were biting back the snappy retorts that hovered just on the edge of their tongues. Kalani took notice of the unspoken exchange, suddenly aware of the soundless expectation of the next round. The phone rang, jolting the three back to a semblance of sanity.

"Jacquelyn Biscayne's office," Kalani found herself whispering into the phone. "Oh sorry, I guess I was whispering. Okay I'll tell her, Matt."

This ought to be good. "That was Matt. He's going to be tied up with Sandro most of the morning and asked if you would drive Ms. Vittore out to the crime scene since you're going out this morning anyway."

Before Jake could answer, Kalani scurried toward the door. "Well, if you two can be trusted not to kill each other, I have work to do."

Cold fury washed through Jake as she made her way to the window, throwing "What next!" out behind her as she felt goosebumps rise on her arms in spite of the heat.

"Damnit!" Cara muttered, fuming with anger and frustration as she headed down the corridor away from Jake's office. It was unnerving how easily the pair had slipped into a hostile, angry relationship. She was suddenly glad that she'd worn heels. Their loud staccato gave her a perverse sense of satisfaction. Every step was like a well-constructed dig at that insufferable woman. Pausing mid-stride, Cara ordered herself to get a grip. Deciding that the only way to make progress on her case was to have a rational conversation with Jake, Cara sighed and returned to the office. However, just because she was acquiescing didn't mean she was going to make it easy for Jake. She walked over to the window and brought her face within inches of the fuming woman.

"Can't we just try to be professionals here? We are on the same side, remember. I've got a kid in jail, your task force still might have a killer on the loose, and all this opposition to me can't be a good use of your energies."

Turning her eyes to meet Cara's gaze, Jake opened her mouth as if to speak, then closed it. Cara could see the internal conflict raging. Then, like a curtain closing and re-opening on a new scene, Jake's eyes conveyed her silent acceptance.

Cara stepped back. "All right then, when do we get started?"

It was Jake who decided to interject a bit of levity into the situation. "Well, if we're going to be working together out at the scene, you've got to lose those heels. I don't think my horse would appreciate them."

"Excuse me? Horse?" Cara looked confused.

"Can you ride, Counselor?" Jake asked, regaining some of her composure.

"Ride?"

"A horse? Can you ride a horse? I want to follow the trail a few miles into the crime site, and the best way to do that is by walking or on horseback. Considering the heat, I prefer horseback. It's your call, Vittore."

"Oh, I think I can manage." The arched eyebrow that accompanied Cara's response was self-explanatory.

Jake gave Cara a disapproving look as her eyes swept over her.

"We'll have to find you some clothes to wear. And boots. I think you might wear the same size as Kal—"

"Don't bother," Cara interrupted and turned toward the door, looking at her watch. "Ten minutes. I'll meet you in the parking lot."

Jake groaned aloud as she reached into her desk for a bottle of ibuprofen. "Great, just how I wanted to spend the day—with an impossible woman in a power suit and heels on horseback. Hell must have finally frozen over."

Impatiently, Jake paced alongside the Land Rover. Standing in the direct sunlight of a July day in Arizona was not a smart thing to do, the sun showed no mercy.

"This is stupid," she muttered to herself, pushing back a stray piece of hair from her face. "Why did I ever agree to this? An old tape clicked on in her brain: *because I am a professional and it's the right thing to do.*

Just then, she spied a transformed Cara approaching. Jake watched the long legs stealthily take in the distance between them. Impossibly long legs sculpted in faded blue jeans and scuffed brown leather boots. A man's long-sleeved denim shirt was open at the neck, and her dark hair was tied loosely at the back of her neck with a red bandanna. Worn leather gloves dangled from her belt, and in one hand she carried a hat that had seen better days. Tearing her eyes away abruptly when Cara flashed her a disarming smile, Jake pivoted around the front of the SUV and mumbled under her breath, "I guess you did manage."

"Let's get going," Jake ordered. "I don't want to stand here too long—the brain starts to sizzle. We'll pick up the horses on the way out of town." She spoke in a dispassionate voice.

Cara called her back, "Let's get one thing straight, Biscayne," she said testily. "I don't take orders from you."

"Oh a bit defensive, aren't we," Jake shot out patronizingly. "Must you take exception to everything I say?"

"Only when you're wrong." Sarcasm colored her voice.

"Well, I'm not wrong here! It's only common sense to get in the truck in the comfort of the air conditioning and get a little relief from this heat," Jake snapped, waving her hand toward the SUV. Between Vittore and the heat, she felt like she was going insane. "Furthermore, I do not intend to stand here and debate the weather with you, Vittore. I need to see the crime scene—*today*. It's hot now, and it sure isn't going to get any cooler where we are going. And if it rains, any evidence we might be lucky enough to find will be washed away."

Shaking her head, Cara breathed heavily. "Why do I get the feeling it's gonna be a long day," she mumbled.

"What was that, Vittore?"

"Okay," throwing her hands up in agreement, "it's hot, so let's get going."

Jake jumped behind the wheel and started the engine. In her haste, she threw the 4x4 in gear just as Cara was climbing in. The jolt hurled Cara precariously against the seat.

"Whoa...hold it. Hold on just a damn minute. Can we just stop this?" Twisting to straighten herself in the seat, Cara inclined her head toward Jake. "Do you come with a warning label— 'hazardous to one's health'?"

Pinching the bridge of her nose, she took a deep breath to regain control of her emotions and smooth her characteristically cool mask back into place. "We both have a job to do," she reminded her. "It's in the best interest of my client and your investigation that we put these petty differences aside. Agreed?"

"Petty differences!" Jake's voice rose as she drilled Cara with her icy eyes. "The differences we have go down to the cellular level, Counselor. There is a basic genetic difference between lawyers and the rest of the human race. And that's as elemental as differences get."

Turning away momentarily, Jake calmed herself and organized her thoughts. This whole situation was bad. It was not a time to be angry. "But I do agree, this isn't helping either one of us." An eerie stillness punctuated by the low hum of the engine settled over them. Jake struggled with her words, obviously uncomfortable. "My anger and your reaction to it only make for clouded judgment and bad investigating. So for right now, I'll try to forget who you are." With resolve Jake said, "Truce...for now."

Cara nodded in agreement. "I can deal with that."

After getting the horses, the two rode in unnerving awkwardness, each still leery of the other. Cara, annoyed by the other woman's determined silence, was just about to launch into some sort of conversation when Jake suddenly pulled into Peña Blanca Canyon, leapt from the truck, and began to unload the horses. Cara followed, pulling on her gloves as she rounded the end of the horse trailer.

"It's down that arroyo about two miles from here," Jake said, nodding her head southward as she lovingly patted the beautiful strawberry roan and backed her out of the trailer.

"This is Soul, my lucky lady," Jake proudly introduced the roan. "You can ride her today, she'll respond to you better. I'll ride Stat since he's a bit more spirited."

"No need," Cara said as she backed Stat out of the trailer, looking him straight in the eyes while rubbing his mane. "We'll get along just fine. Right, boy?"

Half an hour later, the late morning sun beat down mercilessly as the two women traversed a rocky arroyo. The only words spoken were Jake's curt reminders to drink water.

What did you expect, Cara, a day of stimulating conversation? Just be glad she's not yelling at you.

Sweat trickled down her back as she covertly studied the precision and grace with which Jake worked Soul. Rider and horse moved in flawless harmony, anticipating each other perfectly. She considered Jake's lean form—thighs tightly gripping the horse's sides, taut forearm muscles flexing with the slightest curl of her wrist as she directed Soul through the close confines of the brush. Cara was curious about this woman who had infuriated her earlier.

Hmm, I wonder if she and Matt are lovers. With that temper of hers...

She chuckled silently to herself at that thought. Aside from being a force to be reckoned with, the young doctor was also intriguing, smart, and beautiful, an earthy, natural kind of beauty. Her sandy blonde hair woven loosely in a single braid complimented her tan skin. The now hazel eyes softened her features, quite a contrast to the glacial green of a few hours ago. Cara suddenly realized that this woman had elicited a variety of emotions she had not felt in a long time.

The pace picked up as the close scrub and brush thinned into an opening. Jake spurred into a fast canter, leaving Cara behind momentarily. Cara pressed her heels into Stat and galloped to catch up. Just as she was nearing, Soul pulled up abruptly, nostrils flaring, ears laid straight back.

"Whoa, girl. Whoa." Jake spoke softly, leaning forward to rub the roan's neck as she pranced nervously in place. Stat was skittish, too. The animals could smell the rancid stench of death that permeated the desert. They could sense the evil that mingled through the mesquite and willow where the restless spirit of the dead girl stood vigilant. A rustling, mournful tone left a hollow feeling in the air as the wind whished through the green leaves, making the woody branches creak and groan—like the sound of lost souls rushing off to their eternity.

Cara reined Stat in, waiting for Jake to make a move. After a few minutes, Jake swung her leg over the horse and jumped to the ground. Her whole persona changed as the eyes of Dr. Jacquelyn Biscayne, FBI, surveyed the scene below.

"You coming?" Jake absently asked. Cara silently nodded and followed her through the prickly brush into the arroyo. After they squatted outside the yellow tape for what seemed an eternity, Jake's calm, matter-of-fact voice broke the silence and began to paint for Cara a picture of a gruesome, horrific death. Jake possessed an uncanny insight that enabled her to profile a case with remarkable accuracy.

As she expertly worked her way through each detail, Cara couldn't help but admire this woman whose compassion and genuine caring was evident in every word and gesture. Quite a contrast to the willful, combative Jake from a few hours ago. Unanticipated quiet surrounded Cara when Jake finished her account of the evidence. Cara watched as her shoulders slumped, anguish replacing the cavalier bravado.

"Do you think this murder was committed by the same person who killed the other two girls?" Cara asked in a subdued tone.

"I do, and if the evidence supports that theory, then we have a serial killer. I don't believe your client is our killer. From what little I have observed of him, he just does not fit the profile. If he would tell us his name, it would save us a lot of time with his background check. Guess we will have to wait until his prints come back to ID him. We got zilch statewise; hopefully federal will give us something."

Jake shook her head. "I think you should try to delay the arraignment. The guy who did this has a connection to the smuggling of the illegals across the border, and this kid is just that—a kid. It takes a particular kind of sadistic, twisted creature to do what was done to these women...and practice." Jake's voice quivered as she closed her eyes and shook her head sadly. In a strange, unexpected way, Cara wanted to reach out and comfort this challenging woman.

Finding her voice again, Jake continued. "I'm going to follow the trail back toward Mexico a ways. Maybe something—I don't know—anything could be a help in finding this guy. We haven't heard the last from him, I'm afraid, and from what I've seen he enjoys his work...too much. Look, Baltazar will be going back in a little while, just as soon as he finishes up here. You can ride in with him. His trailer will hold Stat," Jake said, looking into Cara's troubled brown eyes.

With no room for debate, Cara simply answered, "I want to go with you."

Jake searched the face looking back at her. "You sure about this? It doesn't get any cooler, and I know I'm not on top of your list for favorite company."

"I'm positive. We made it this far without shedding blood. I think we can, hmm, let me see, behave, don't you? Besides, I can take a little heat." Cara grinned.

Jake raised a dubious eyebrow, trying to contain a small smile. "We'll see...I guess it would be okay." Looking over to where her friend and fellow agent was finishing loading the equipment, she said, "I'll tell Baltazar, then we can get going while there are still a few good hours of daylight left."

Chapter Four

Remounting their horses, the women turned south toward Mexico. The late-afternoon sun was cruel and unforgiving, literally sucking the moisture from both horse and rider. Jake knew it wasn't a good idea to go on this time of day, especially with the percussion of distant thunder closing in on them.

"We better stop a while and water the horses, let them cool down a bit." She stroked Soul's neck before slipping from the saddle, feeling the hot lather the horse had worked up.

Within minutes, the day turned sultry as scorching heat mixed with wet air. In spite of being shaded by the brimmed hat she wore, sweat glistened on Jake's tan face and ran into her eyes. Her drenched shirt clung to her body like a second skin. Pulling a bandanna from her back pocket, she removed her hat and wiped the inside of the brim. Wetting the cloth from the water bag, she rubbed the back of her neck and squeezed water down her shirt in between her breasts. She let out a blustering sigh of relief before tying the cool cloth around her throat. Studying the churning clouds as they released wispy grey rain that dissipated before it hit the ground, both riders watched the signs of the monsoon thunderstorm sweep toward them.

The first gust of wind ruffled Jake's hair as she pointed toward the west. "Monsoon clouds. It won't be long before the hammer strikes the anvil. We need to turn back and get out of the arroyo now." Disappointment shadowed her face. "Guess we won't find anything more out here after the rain hits."

Cara was no stranger to the perils of the late-summer monsoon rains and knew Jake was right. A dry riverbed or gulch could transform into a torrent of raging water before you even saw it coming. She recalled reading about several experienced hikers losing their lives in the Grand Canyon when they were caught unexpectedly in a flash flood. The sky darkened ominously as storm clouds pushed closer, gathering strength. A streak of lightening flashed off to the west toward the Pajarito Mountains. It wouldn't be long now.

"You said this was the only body found in this arroyo?" Cara asked, still intently mindful of the skyline.

"Yes. The other two were deeper in the desert, southwest of here at California Gulch. It's right at the border, but they were on our side of the line. This entire area, from Peña Blanca on west to Sasabe, is a known area for illegal crossings, so we have every reason to suspect that they are somehow associated. I can't help but question how many more have there been that the desert or the animals claimed that we don't even know about. And what about on the other side of the line—how many has he dumped there? I damn well know there have to be more."

"You are certain these murders are connected to the smugglers?" Cara's analytical mind was working overtime.

"As certain as I can be. This last one, and the fact that we were able to recover more evidence, pieced it together better. I believe the connection is there and the killer picks his victims from unsuspecting women who try to cross illegally."

Cara's eyes grew critical. "What was the scene like where the other two bodies were found?"

"More remote, in a flatter area than these rolling hills—it's hotter, dryer. Nocturnal predator and scavenger activity is greater. By the time we found those girls, there wasn't enough left of them to make any sure determination as to the cause of death. They looked like roadkill." Jake hesitated as the picture coalesced in her mind. "Have you ever seen what a pack of javelina and a few starving coyotes can do to a body?" Her voice was barely audible. "Believe me, it is not a pretty sight. Everything was so badly decomposed or contaminated by scavengers that the DNA samples were useless."

Jake's thoughts flashed back to the trial and the DNA evidence Cara so expertly had dismissed. She grew silent, withdrawn from the conversation and lost in thought. It disturbed her, and Cara sensed it.

Not wanting to lose the developing rapport by treading on touchy ground, Cara took a sip of water, deliberately avoiding the term *DNA*. "Tell me what you think."

"So now you're interested in what I think," Jake countered in a voice that was sharp and testy, like a stubborn child's.

Cara looked her straight in the eye. "Yes." She paused for another swallow of water. "I want to know what your gut instinct is telling you about this guy."

"Why?"

"Because that kid in jail is depending on you. The families of these girls are depending on you. Because I'm depending on you."

With each word, the sense of urgency was clearly evident in her tone. Although Jake thought Cara offered that last bit of information a little bit too readily, she also recognized the woman's sincerity. She hesitated for a moment, fanning her face with her hat. "I would like to think that you can trust me."

"That's good. I need to know if you trust me as well. I realize that might be difficult." Cara's voice had turned solemn.

Jake looked up at a tall cottonwood, pondering. *What other choice do I have?*

"I trust you. But only because I have to," she replied frankly.

"Well, that's honest," Cara acknowledged. "So. What do you think?"

"He's someone who blends in, able to travel back and forth across the border without drawing attention to himself. Possibly Hispanic, could be an American citizen. Then again, he might be a Mexican citizen who does a legal business this side of the border."

Jake remounted and shifted in the saddle, gazing out at the desert landscape. "What do you see out there?"

Cara followed Jake's gaze, looking out at the unspoiled Sonoran desert. Everything was in its place. Even the clouds were amassing predictably. Cara understood what Jake was telling her. "I see what belongs here."

"Exactly. Our killer believes he is above suspicion. He knows this area as well as I do, and I grew up here, so that's pretty damn well. He knows this desert, how its deceptive serenity can camouflage bodies along with any immediate trace evidence long enough for the elements and the scavengers to obliterate it altogether. Take this last one, for example. The monsoons are a week late. We should have been in the thick of it. Now, almost a week after the discovery of the body, there's still no rain. We've been able to cover the scene with a fine-tooth comb before anything washed away. Mother Nature threw us a lucky break, and I plan to use it to catch this bastard. Nogales will not become another Juárez."

Listening to the conviction in Jake's voice as she continued her profile, Cara found herself admiring the feisty doctor.

"The actual figure of illegals crossing the two-thousand-mile border into the States each year would stagger your imagination. So far this year, we've had over a hundred deaths here in the Tucson Sector. Even the new sensors don't stop them from coming. There's an old wagon trail just south of here, the *Camino del Diablo*, the Devil's Highway. It parallels the international border and is a notorious crossing zone. Yet, even with a name like that, its reputation for being the death of so many, they still come like lemmings racing to their deaths. Especially this time of year, and so many die from heat exhaustion or dehydration. But a woman will seldom if ever brave the elements by herself. And it's most unlikely she would be left to die alone. That tells me that these women were targeted, separated somehow from the rest, beaten, brutalized, raped, and left for the desert to clean up. Our killer has sadistic inclinations, and I don't think he's your average *coyote* or *pollero*. And he's certainly not a simple *sacadinero* who's covering up his double-dealing."

Cara unconsciously clenched her fingers into fists, the muscles in her jaw working as Jake spoke. "So we're dealing with an efficient killing machine that's hiding right under our noses. And he's been getting away with it too long."

"Or so he thinks—who knew the monsoons would be this late, allowing us to gather as much evidence as we have? Especially the DNA we recovered. He's made mistakes, Vittore; they all do, no matter how clever and devious they think they are. I just have to find it. That one piece of evidence that will nail him. This time, it feels different."

"Jake, did you ever read Poe?"

"Poe, as in Edgar Allen, as in 'The Raven' and 'Annabel Lee'? Sure, but just what's that got to do with anything?"

"Right guy, wrong works. Seems Mr. Poe, the inventor of ratiocination, better known as the detective story, proposed in his book *The Purloined Letter* that the best way to hide something is in plain sight."

Jake found herself listening to Cara's voice, and to her surprise, enjoying it. *I can't believe I am out here in the desert, with her, discussing literature and this case like we were old friends or something.* She suddenly was jolted out of deep thought by Soul's change in gate. She was limping, favoring her right.

"What's wrong with Soul?" Cara asked as she rode up to Jake.

"I don't know, must have picked up something in her shoe. We better pull up over there." Jake pointed to a clump of mesquite as she headed for one exceptionally large, canopied tree. She was watching her surroundings, carefully easing past the thorny reaches of the close-growing mesquite when she heard Stat's familiar warning snort. Before she could turn around in the tight confines of the shrubs, Jake recognized the comical gruntings of the pig-like javelina before she saw them. Cougars were common in the area so the javelina were actually a welcome sound. If there were javelina, it was a safe bet there were no cougars. Stat didn't agree; he reared at the underbrush intruders into his otherwise peaceful world. Just as Jake had turned Soul toward her back trail, she saw Stat rush headlong into the thorny fingers of mesquite branches that clawed and grabbed at both horse and rider.

"Just duck low and hang on, Cara," Jake shouted above the confusion and sound of breaking branches and the squeals of frightened little javelina piglets. When she placed two fingers in her mouth and gave a shrill, two-toned warbling kind of whistle, Stat responded instantly and came to a dead stop.

Cara jumped to the ground. Her first instinct was to check the horse for cuts or other injuries, an action that was not lost on the ever-observant Jake.

As Jake neared, she could see blood running from Cara's left side. The mesquite thorns had done a good job of shredding her shirt and the skin underneath. Jake sprang from the saddle and rushed up to Cara. "Are you all right? Damn, you look a mess."

Without looking up from her inspection of the horse, Cara grimaced as she spoke. "I'm fine, looks like Stat is too."

Jake walked slowly over to her horse so as not to spook him any more than he was already and whispered low into his ear. "You okay, boy?" Her tanned hands ran along his mane and neck. The horse had fared well with the exception of some minor scrapes.

"He's good, aren't ya fella? But," looking at the blood soaking through what was left of Cara's shirt, "you are another story. Here, let me see that cut," Jake ordered as she snatched off her bandanna to wipe the blood away.

"I'm fine, stop fussing. It's just a few scratches."

"You know what, Vittore, I'll be the judge of that. So quit trying to impress me with the macho routine, okay?"

She turned the lawyer around to get a closer look at the damage. Lifting the torn shirt, Jake could see the gash on the smooth skin below Cara's ribs.

"Cara, I need to get you back to the clinic. This is a fairly deep laceration. It may need a few stitches. When was your last tetanus shot?"

"Oh no, you're not getting near me with a needle!" Cara retorted, with more than just a little fear in her voice.

"What? You don't mean to tell me that the great Cara Vittore, lawyer extraordinaire, is afraid of a little ole shot, do you?"

"I'm not afraid of anything. It's just not necessary is all. I'll be fine."

"Right. Whatever you say. But who's the doctor here? And I say you need stitches and a tetanus shot. Mesquite cuts can get infected very quickly, Cara."

Jake pressed the makeshift dressing into the wound to stop the bleeding before tying her belt around it to keep it in place. "Come on, hot shot, let's get going."

Jake kept an eye on the threatening monsoon clouds. Jagged flashes of lightening and the rumbling thunder were bearing down on them. The sky was turning an eerie gold and grey. Even though it wasn't raining where they were, the water that was already falling in the mountains above them would soon make its way to them, transforming the dry arroyo into a raging river.

They were about a mile from the trailer with Jake leading the way and Cara trailing. Cara hadn't hurt much at first, probably due to the pain-killing effects of an adrenaline rush, but now her body ached all over. The wounds from the thorny mesquite felt like razor cuts, and blood was oozing through the bandanna and running down her hip. Jake slowed her pace to let Stat come up alongside.

"We're going to ride up out of the arroyo the rest of the way," pointing to the mountains to the north. "Won't be long before the water comes."

Suddenly, a movement in the brush behind Cara caught Jake's eye. "Over your shoulder," came the controlled whisper. "Something, no someone, is hiding in the brush."

"I know, I spotted them just as you slowed up."

Jake eased the weapon she carried in the field from the holster at her waist and looked at Cara with intense eyes. "Well, whoever it is they are not very good at it. A deaf person could hear 'em," Jake whispered.

"How do you want to do this, Jake?"

"You, stay put!" she hissed through her teeth as she heeled Soul and took off in a flurry of dust and flying dirt clods toward the brush before Cara could say a word.

Damn, she is an irritating woman! "Stay put." I don't think so, lady.

Cara veered off in the opposite direction, riding hard to cut around the side where Jake would flush out the intruder. Just as she reached a clearing, a figure ran from the brush directly in front of Stat causing him to rear up, his forelegs flailing in an attempt to ward off the danger. Cara expertly sat the horse, leaning into his neck while reining him down. His hooves landed inches away from the figure lying motionless on the ground. Vaulting from the saddle, she was just kneeling down beside the curled-up form as Jake arrived.

"It's just a boy!" yelled Cara incredulously, bending down to see if he was hurt.

Jake crouched beside Cara, bewildered. She was too concerned for the child for her anger at Cara to register. "A boy? Is he all right?" she questioned as she reached to examine him.

"Do not hurt me, *por favor*." The boy, obviously Hispanic, was about eight or so. He held his arms protectively over his head. Dirty tatters of clothing hung loosely on his thin, shaking frame.

"Are you hurt? What are you doing out here? Are you alone?" Jake questioned.

"*Diablo! Diablo!*" His frightened brown eyes darted back and forth between the two women.

"Easy...easy. It's all right, we're not going to hurt you. Can you stand up? Do you understand me?" Cara asked in a soothing voice, trying to calm the boy.

The small, frightened figure cowered back, arms extended as if to ward off an evil monster that was about to devour him.

At the same time, both women were startled by the noise speeding toward them from behind and turned to see a man running at them frantically with a staff raised to strike. Before Jake could draw her weapon, one swift movement from Cara disarmed the intruder and a second had him pinned to the ground with her boot pressed against his throat. The boy flung himself at Cara, pounding his fists against her, screaming in a desperate attempt to protect the man on the ground.

"*Padre! Padre!*"

"Father? This is your father?" Cara questioned, releasing her hold on the man's throat.

The crying boy ran into his father's arms. "*Padre. Padre.*"

"Miguel!" The man cried as he hugged the child tightly. I'm here, do not cry, little one. I'm here. No one will harm you."

Cara and Jake stood silently watching the distraught father and son. After the boy had quieted down, Jake asked, "What are you doing out here, are you lost, how did you get here?"

The man's eyes darted between the pistol at Jake's waist and the water bag hanging from the saddle. Warily he asked, "You are BP? You will send us back?"

Jake felt the first touch of cooling rain on her face. She understood the defeat in the man's sad eyes and regretted the answer to the question. "The first thing we need to do is get you and your son to safety and medical attention. This wash will not be dry for long. Then we'll talk," Jake said as she untied the water bag, knelt down beside the boy, and motioned for him to drink as the rain began to fall harder. Panic closed over the man's face.

"*Señorita*! There is danger here from the fast water?"

"*Sí.* This is a flash flood area. This whole wash, dry as it is now, can turn into a torrent of water in a matter of minutes. We'll be on high ground long before the water comes," Jake quickly said, trying to calm his fear.

"I must go! Please, *señorita*, take my boy. Please, please keep him safe," the man pleaded as trembling hands pushed the young child toward the two women. "Go with them, Miguel."

An unmistakable tenor of desperation tinged the man's voice as he turned and anxiously looked toward the direction he had come from. Rain was cascading down his face now, and he straightened his slumped shoulders. The strength of his voice contrasted with his frail and exhausted appearance as he declared, "I must hurry."

Cara sensed the man's urgency. "Where are you going? Why are you so frightened?" She reached out and touched him gently on his arm. "Let us help you. Please."

The man hesitated only a moment before answering. "My family, *señorita*, they are in the arroyo. They do not know the danger from the water! I told them to stay while I went to find Miguel. I need to go back. To help them to safety, please, *señorita*, let me go to them before the water comes!"

Cara looked to Jake, who was already lifting the boy onto Soul.

"You ride with Cara," Jake directed the man. "We need to hurry!" She unclipped the cell phone from her belt and pushed the number for the Nogales Border Patrol.

"Eduardo, this is Jake. I am approximately two miles up the wash from the crime scene at Smuggler's Gulch. We have a man and his son with us. We're on horseback. His wife and..." yelling back to the man, "how many, *señor*, how many are there?"

"*Tres, señorita, tres,* my wife and daughters."

"Three," Jake repeated to Eduardo. "He was separated from his wife and two children. We're on the way to find them before it turns into a river down here. Can you get a helicopter out to pick them up? It looks like they have been hiding out here a few days, probably all in need of medical attention."

"It's raining and blowing pretty hard, Jake. Visibility is near zero, and the winds are gusting to fifty, but we'll try. You say you're two miles up Smuggler's Gulch? Headed south?"

"Yeah, that's where we're at right now, I don't know how far in his family is, but he's on foot so I'm hoping not too far."

"Okay, keep your phone on. If we can get a chopper up, we'll get a fix on you and then go to look for them."

"They're illegals, Eduardo, so they might be hiding, especially from a BP helicopter."

"We need to find them, pronto. It won't be long before you'll all be swimming. Jake, you know when to get out, right?"

"Right, Eduardo. With a little luck we'll find them fast."

The rain was pelting the four riders now with a vengeance. The sky, dark and angry, verbalized its displeasure and power with flashes of lightening chased by long, earth-trembling rumbles.

"I don't know! I don't know!" the man cried, "this looks like the place, but I am not sure."

Frantically, he called into the echoes of thunder, "Rosa! Rosa!" But only hollow whisper of rain splattering against dry rocks answered him.

Jake kept an anxious eye on the wash behind them. *It won't be long. We need to get up out of the wash. Damn, where are they, where are they?*

Cara pulled Stat up as if reading Jake's mind. "Take the boy and his father to higher ground, Jake. I can go faster by myself. Besides, your chopper should be here any minute now."

"Not on your life, Vittore. This is my responsibility, not yours. You take them and get to safety, I'll keep looking."

Glacier green eyes locked into equally determined brown ones that were unflinching. *Come on, this is no time to decide you might actually like this woman,* Jake thought. *Is she grandstanding or just plain nuts?*

"We're wasting time here, Jake, don't argue."

Just then, the howling wind and noise of helicopter blades whirred overhead. Matt's amplified voice emerged from the clamor.

"We have them! Get out of there, Jake, now!"

Eduardo and Matt looked desperately for a place where the riders could climb out of the wash, but the walls of the gulch were too steep and muddy. They circled to see how close the raging torrent of water was.

Eduardo's jaw dropped in disbelief. "Holy shit, it's almost on top of them, Matt."

"Goddamn! They're not going to make it!"

Spinning the chopper around for a better look, Eduardo sighted a possibility.

"Look, Matt, over there! See that trail, they can get a foothold on the rocks!"

The chopper hovered as Matt yelled into the mike, "Jake, fifty yards ahead to your right. Go! It's breathing down your neck!"

Jake shouted to Cara, her heart pounding out of her chest, as they rode frantically searching for a way out. "Ahead fifty yards."

She tightened her arms around the small boy in front of her and spurred Soul into a gallop toward the trail. Cara followed with her passenger hanging on for dear life. Jake was half way up the trail when she heard the roar behind her. Just as she crested the top of the wash to safety, she heard Cara shouting, "Grab something and hang on!"

Still holding tight to the boy, Jake turned in the saddle to follow the path of the searchlight. At the edge of the gully, she saw the boy's father. He was bobbing only inches above the floodwaters, clinging to an overhanging tree branch.

"God no, please no," Jake cried out desperately as her eyes blindly searched the raging black water for Cara and Stat. The piercing glare of the searchlight did little to illuminate the surrounding darkness. Within minutes, the buffeting turbulence from the helicopter forced her to dismount as it landed on the plateau of the arroyo. Miguel was sobbing and calling for his father. As Jake looked into the nothingness, agonizing helplessness and anguish engulfed her. Matt and Eduardo quickly tossed a line to the man and pulled him to safety. Tears brimmed his eyes while his words poured out in broken English.

"Gracias, gracias, señorita, God bless you. You and your friend, *mi familia,* you save them."

Hesitantly touching Jake's hand, he spoke in a heartfelt tone that ripped through her like a knife. "I-I am sorry, *señorita.* The lady, how you say, she was *valerosa,* brave."

Then he was gone, rushing to his wife and children who were huddled outside the chopper. Jake was numbly aware of father, mother, and children reuniting in a tearful embrace.

As she turned back toward the shadows, her only conscious thought was that Cara was gone. The woman she had damned for so long had risked her life trying to help her and total strangers.

Matt plainly saw what was on Jake's mind as she wheeled toward him. "Now, Jake, it's—"

"Don't you 'now Jake, me,' Matt Peyson," she spat. Her eyes watered as she pled, "Please, Matt, we need to find them. Maybe they made it. Can't we at least make a pass down the wash?"

Matt scanned Jake's tormented face. He'd seen her under every circumstance imaginable but he had only seen her as shaken as she was right now once before, and that was after the murders of Sam and her father. He knew it was dangerous flying in this weather and that they should wait it out until it cleared a bit. But when did he ever have common sense where she was concerned? He never could refuse her anything. Besides, it was the right thing to do. Looking to Eduardo to make the call, Matt got a thumbs-up from the pilot.

"There isn't enough room in the chopper for all of us," Matt apologized, motioning to the family huddled in the rain.

"They're safe enough where they are, and they can hold Soul for you until BP gets a rescue team in here."

Not wasting any more time, Matt and Eduardo hastily strung a canvas shelter to protect the family from the pelting rain while Jake tended her horse.

"Let's go!" Matt yelled, and he grabbed Jake's hand, pulling her into the chopper.

A brilliant shaft of light penetrated the night, darting across the water's blackness for any sign of horse or rider. Uprooted trees and debris were strewn everywhere, but there was no sign of Cara or Stat. Seeing Jake in the pale glow of the instrument panel, Matt knew he loved her and had since they were teenagers riding through the rolling Santa Cruz hills. Yet, he was helpless to comfort her now. She loved Stat, and losing him was going to be traumatic enough. Even worse, he could see in her eyes how she was berating herself for allowing Cara to be in harm's way.

"Nothing," Matt shouted, wiping the rain from his face with his hand while hanging halfway out of the helicopter. "It's too damn dark, and this rain is coming down so hard I can't see past my nose. We gotta go, Jake. I'll check in with the rescue team, but in this weather I dunno, won't see much until daylight."

"No! Please! We have to keep looking. She might be hurt...they...might need help. Please, Matt, just a little longer."

Eduardo, who had been eyeing the fuel gage, called back to Matt. "We're running on fumes, boss. Sorry, Jake, but we gotta go, now."

Jake let out a defeated breath as Matt gave the order. "Take it home, Eduardo."

Jake stared out the window, silent tears streaming down her face like the rain running down the window of the chopper. She felt numb. The last twelve hours seemed surreal. Was it only that morning the anxiety and anger she felt toward Cara Vittore was all consuming? That anger had festered unreasonably for two years, and tonight Vittore was gone and probably dead, because of her.

Why did I let her come with me, why? It's all my fault, a civilian for God's sake. Didn't I learn the last time, wasn't there enough pain and guilt? She moaned and covered her face with her hands. *Oh, Stat, I am so sorry.*

When the chopper landed, Matt insisted on driving her home but she refused, needing to be alone. She took one of the Border Patrol trucks and drove out to her ranch at Rio Rico. All she wanted was to forget the ache and loss she felt in her heart for a woman whom she had hated but really didn't know. Painful memories were too close to the surface, memories she could not allow. Oblivious to her muddy, wet clothes she stumbled into bed, praying for sleep.

Chapter Five

Merciless heat knifed at the exposed flesh of her hands. She had no sense of direction. There was no up, no down. Precariously, she dangled above leaping flames that snaked upward, raking her face with fiery claws and lashing her body in flaming ropes. Thrashing at the stinging fingers that were drawing her into the vortex of molten lava, she saw a face. There, in the glowing center of the untouchable, white-hot river was...was Cara! Not Sam, but Cara! The face, the voice kept changing. But not the desperate eyes, pleading eyes. The mantra-like voice tortured her, accusing, demanding why. *I trusted you, help me— please help me.* Jake hysterically battled the flames, striving to embrace the voice. But the image was elusive, always just beyond her grasp. Screaming. It was her voice! Her heart was racing, pounding out of her chest; she was running now. Burning shreds of flesh evaporated into the inferno as the voice penetrated the darkness, the smoke, the flames, inexorably summoning her. Hot winds of fear sucked air from her lungs as she crawled toward the voice. Behind her in the distance, she heard Matt.

"Jake, open up, open up. Jake, it's Matt!" he yelled, pounding on the door. "Let me in."

Jake awoke, still dazed. She couldn't remember how she had gotten home or why her clothes were damp. The realization hit her all at once; she moaned, clutching the pillow to her face.

"Oh God, Cara." She sat up and pulled her knees to her chest, rocking back and forth, trying not to remember.

Matt's lean, strong-boned face peered into the kitchen through the window. Seeing no movement, he loped around the side of the house to the veranda off Jake's bedroom. The door was unlocked, and he stepped into the room. Jake looked up, but her empty eyes stared past him, seemingly unaware of his presence. When Matt sat beside her and touched her lightly on the shoulder, she turned lifelessly toward him. For a long moment he said nothing at all, and when he did speak, his voice was tender and caring.

"It wasn't your fault, Jake. You know how the washes flood. You—"

"Don't you dare try to blame this just on the weather and how unpredictable the washes are!" she lashed out. "I knew better. I should never have had her out there in the first place."

The unexpectedness of Jake's belligerent tone took him off guard. Matt stood and walked to the window, watching the gathering clouds in the slate-grey sky as the winds whipped dust upward in spirals. There was something comforting about the summer storms, even in their brutality.

"So are you just gonna hole up in this house and die all over again because you couldn't control the situation?"

"Why not?" Jake said coldly.

Refusing to let Jake wallow in self-pity and misplaced guilt, he took an equally hard tone with her.

"Come on, Jake, snap out of it. It was not your fault, you hear me? Jesus Christ, woman, this is a hard land and you know these things can and do happen. Cara was there because she wanted to be there. You did not cause this. And are you forgetting that if you hadn't been out there, that entire family would have been swept away?"

The overwrought doctor struggled to regain composure. In a parched voice she asked, "How are they, Matt? Is everyone okay?" Her lifeless eyes suddenly filled with fear. "Soul, where is Soul?"

"Calm down, they're all okay and being treated at the hospital for dehydration. The young boy seems traumatized. He just clings to his dad, but they are all doing fine. Soul's in the corral now. I wanted to make sure you got home all right last night so I followed you out. I brought her home and put her in the barn so she'd be out of the rain and here when you got up."

Pulling her up off the bed, Matt observed, "You look a mess. Go shower and change. I'll put on some coffee."

Jake wiped her eyes on her sleeve and headed toward the bathroom. She stopped, turning back toward Matt, her face dirty and tear-stained. "Thank you for being such a good friend."

Matt saw only the beautiful, sad eyes of the woman he had loved for as long as he could remember. He walked over and put his arms around her, holding her gently and resting his chin on her head.

"I love you, Jake."

Allowing herself only a moment of comfort in Matt's arms, she pulled away. "I know, Matt. I know."

Sipping his coffee, Matt sat in the front porch rocker with his boots hooked over the railing. He heard the rattle of cups and coffeepot from the kitchen and knew Jake had finished her shower. When she joined him outside, he glanced quickly in her direction. She had dressed in jeans, boots, and a chambray shirt. Her hair, still damp, hung loosely about her shoulders. A curious emptiness filled his stomach. He was in love with her. She was all he wanted, all he could ever want. Yet he sat quietly helpless, unable to soothe her agony, and watched her gaze sadly out toward the rolling green hills and the Santa Rita Mountains in the distance.

Jake had always felt the power of the incredible beauty that surrounded her. The tranquility and healing powers of the Sonoran Desert were the main reasons she transferred home to the Nogales/Tucson sector. This land and its mystic effect had helped heal her tormented soul and with time, an acceptable peace had infused her heart. But today, all that was gone. The harmony and quietude did nothing to diminish the ache in her heart. Wracked with sorrow, she felt helpless as old wounds opened to expose painful memories. Feeling queasy from the coffee, Jake set her cup down, picked up a leather strap from the table, and tied her hair back.

"I want to go up in the chopper. Will you call Eduardo and have him pick me up here?"

"Whoa! Jake, you're exhausted. You don't need to be out there today. The rescue teams and BP are out in full force." The minute the words were out, he knew it was the wrong thing to say.

Jake turned to face Matt, the determination written on her face. "I *will* see this through, and I *will* go up today. And if you won't call Eduardo, I will," she said resolutely.

Matt seemed about to speak, but his cell phone interrupted the mounting confrontation. Jake walked to the door with quick, purposeful steps to get her phone.

"Hold up, Jake."

She turned her grave and quiet eyes to stare at Matt as he held the phone to his ear, but the look on his face caused her to step forward.

"What is it, Matt?" A cold shiver ran through Jake's body, and her face paled. "Have they found them?"

"We'll be right there, Eduardo."

A slow, crooked grin spread upward from the corners of Matt's mouth. He rubbed his chin as he watched Jake's eyes fill with startled comprehension.

"Yep, they found her, or rather she found *them*. She just walked into the ranger station out on Ruby Road, looking pretty banged up, leading a limping horse. Hustle it up, lady, she might be needing a doctor."

Eduardo relayed the message back to the ranger station. "Matt and Jake are on the way over, Karl. You sure she doesn't want us to transport her to Tucson Medical Center to be checked out?"

Karl glanced out the window as he spoke. "We suggested it, Ed, downright insisted on it. But she insisted in no uncertain terms that she wasn't going anywhere."

He blushingly remembered Cara's colorful way of saying no. "She's alert, bruised up everywhere, got a wound on her side, a gash on her head, and right now she is out looking the horse over for injuries! So, if Matt and Jake want to take her to a hospital—good luck. They can tackle this one."

Eduardo chuckled. "Shouldn't be long before they get there. Let Jake handle her."

Cara stroked the horse's mane while talking quietly into his ear.

"We made it boy, some ride, huh."

She ran her hands down his hind legs, inspecting them for injuries, then moved to his forelegs. Lifting Stat's right front hoof, she detected the swelling around his fetlock and a slight split in the hoof.

"Looks like we're both intact, fella, nothing broken anyway. This leg will be just fine as soon as we get you to a doc."

The horse snorted and pushed his nose into her side. Cara grimaced in pain. Turning pale, she held her left rib area as she slowly exhaled the breath she had been holding. Startled by the familiar voice behind her, she turned to see an indignant Jake standing there.

"What do you think you're doing?" Jake asked.

Underneath the outward appearance of anger, Cara read the relief in her face. Wordlessly, their eyes exchanged the emotions they could not voice. Cara forgot the pain in her side, and Jake was holding back tears of mixed emotions.

Walking slowly over to Cara, Jake touched her cheek. "I'm glad you're all right I-I...thought you..."

Cara felt herself blushing. "Hey, remember me, the lawyer from hell? I'm too ornery to get hurt."

She held Jake's hand to her cheek as she whispered close to her ear. "I'm glad you made it, too."

It was Jake's turn to hold her breath. Consciously ignoring the light-headedness that Cara's whisper elicited, she turned on her heels, tugging the injured woman behind her.

"Come on, I want to see what you've done to yourself and look at that wound on your side."

"But I'm all righ—"

"Don't even say it, Vittore."

Sitting in the medic office of the ranger station, Cara flinched when Jake palpated her left side.

"Well, Ms. Nothing-can-hurt-me-I'm-tough-as-nails, you probably have two fractured ribs. The wound on your side is—surprise—infected and needs stitching, so does this gash on your head. You're one big bruise, and you're going to hurt like hell tomorrow...if you don't already. You need a megadose of antibiotics. And a tetanus shot."

"Are you finished now?" Cara asked, trying to take in a deep breath. "I am *not,* repeat *not* going to a hospital. I have a perfectly good doctor right here in the room with me. You can do all of the above and let me go home!"

"Cara, you need x-rays to see if a rib has punctured your lung. You're having trouble breathing. You can't even take in a deep breath." With her hands on her hips, she glared at Cara. "Don't be so stubborn."

"I am not going to TMC, Jake, and that's final. We can go to your office, you have the equipment there, and you can enjoy stitching me up and poking me with those needles of yours. End of story, take it or let me be on my way," Cara said with difficulty, trying to catch her breath.

Jake entertained the idea of letting her do just that. Feeling the old, familiar annoyance, she punctuated every word of her sentence. "You...are... the most...annoying...and irritating...and totally exasperating woman I have ever met!"

Holding up her hands in mock surrender, she continued, "But, and I do mean but, if you will let me do my work, with your mouth *shut,* and agree to stay at my ranch for a few days so I can keep an eye on you, I will go along with your craziness. Deal?"

Cara studied Jake's face, feeling too tired and weak to argue. Reluctantly, through pain-whitened lips, she managed a raspy, "One night, I'll stay one night."

Even though Jake could handle the x-rays and suturing in her office, her better judgment told her that Cara really should have gone to TMC for observation and treatment. Yet, there had been no arguing with the obstinate woman. She was relieved when the x-ray revealed no rib fractures. If it had, she had no idea how she would have convinced Cara to go to the hospital, especially after the numerous oaths she had endured regarding her motives with all the needles.

On the drive out to the ranch, Jake watched Cara sleeping in the seat next to her. A sedative had helped ease the pain enough for her to relax and drift off. The dim light of dusk played across Cara's face. It was just enough, however, to let Jake continue in her unobserved study of the woman beside her.

Hmm, asleep she looks so...so what, Jake? You've condemned this woman for the past two years for something that was your fault. She was right, it was your error that got the DNA evidence thrown out. I shouldn't have been back to work so soon after the accident. But...she's still a priceless pain in the ass. No doubt about it, she is an irritating woman. A fascinating one but impossible. Listen to yourself, Jake, rationalizing your feelings. Your hands were shaking so bad when you sewed her up it's a wonder she didn't beg you to take her to the hospital right then and there. She's the one who was hurt, but you were the one who couldn't breathe. Oh! And don't forget how your heart tripped over itself when she was close enough to feel her breath on your neck. Be honest, you misjudged this woman. You like her, and you don't know how to eat crow.

Jake shook Cara gently when they arrived at the ranch. "Hey, we're here. How does a soft bed sound?"

An unintelligible grumble was the only response from the sedated, exhausted woman.

"Okay, looks like you need a little help there."

Going around to the passenger side, wrapping her arms around Cara's waist, carefully avoiding the sensitive ribs, she eased her out of the SUV. "Come on, tough guy."

Cara rolled over on her good side, boots and all, after Jake deposited her onto the bed in the guestroom.

"Cara, can you wake up and get undressed? Hey." She shook her gently. "Cara?"

Jake stood perplexed, wondering what do about Cara's dirty, bloody clothes.

Now, if I had insisted she go to a hospital I wouldn't be standing here like a damn intern, at a loss as to whether or not she could just sleep in her wet clothes, now would I? Nervously, she debated. *Well, I guess I can at least take off the muddy boots.*

Jake gently rolled Cara onto her back and tugged off one boot and then the other. Her socks were still damp, saturated with mud, as were her jeans.

"Now what?" Jake's eyes traveled up Cara's body. She had cleaned and stitched the wounds on Cara's side and head back at the office, but the woman's impatience hadn't allowed Jake time to clean the superficial cuts on her upper body and arms. They needed an antibiotic ointment applied; besides, the wet clothes needed to come off.

Come on, you just can't let her lay there all night in wet clothes, you're a doctor, Jake, so get with it. She's flesh and blood just like everyone else, right? Huh uh, sure she is! Well, bite the bullet and get over it! You agreed, no hospital, so roll your sleeves up before pneumonia sets in.

She stood a moment longer looking down at the enigmatic woman who now appeared so vulnerable and actually seemed...human.

Even after all she's been through, dirty, torn clothes and all, she is—yes, she is beautiful! I wonder what's behind those sad eyes?

Jake mentally censured her thoughts, shrugged, and went to gather a basin and towels. She bathed Cara's bruised body, cleansing the minor wounds and applying Neosporin here and there. Finished, she pulled the quilt over the sleeping olive-skinned woman, dimmed the light, then wearily walked down the hall to her room for some much-needed rest.

After settling Cara in, Jake slept through the evening hours and well into the night, until the sound of hard rain on the tile roof woke her. She went to the guestroom to check on Cara, who was still sleeping soundly. Fully awake now, she brewed a pot of her favorite Sumatra blend coffee and went out to the veranda to watch the spectacular lightening display in the night sky. She loved the Arizona lightening storms. They were a breathtaking show of nature's power. She could feel the potentially dangerous raw energy of the storm encroaching with each jagged flash of white light that reached angrily across the blue-black horizon. The air was heavy with humidity, and the darkness crackled with electricity. The night and all things in it seemed to be holding their collective breath, waiting another onslaught of the building storm.

Jake sipped her coffee as another bolt of light lit the night sky. A low voice from behind nudged her from her solitude.

"Beautiful, isn't it. Makes one feel in awe and quite insignificant."

Jake turned to see Cara leaning against the frame of the Spanish archway of the veranda in her bare feet and the man's pajama top she'd laid at the foot of the bed.

"Hey you, you're supposed to be in bed resting," Jake said in a tender voice.

"Seems I have been. Looks like I slept through what was left of the day and most of the night." She looked down at the nightshirt with a grin. "Thank you for...well, all your care last night," Cara teased.

Jake felt the blush creeping up her neck and face as she stood up.

Hmm, so she did undress and wash me. Ah! Jake, that is a very interesting color.

"Well I didn't want to get the bedspread dirty, now did I? Who else was going to undress and clean you up, Counselor? Hmm, do you see anyone else around here? So you can just take that smirk off your face. After all I am a...a doctor." *Damn! I always seem to feel like a raving loon around her. Well, tit for tat.* "Besides, you had mud in some mighty interesting places."

This time Cara's face flushed bright red. Smiling shyly, she asked, "Uh...um...uh, would it be okay to take a shower...I mean, with this dressing? I think a good share of that mud is still in my hair."

Cara's dark eyes warmed as she touched Jake on the shoulder. "Sincerely, thank you for all your care and opening your home to me, Jake."

The same odd sensation Jake had felt the day before when she first saw Cara with Stat in the corral at the ranger station arced through her...a funny catch deep inside her chest. She lowered her eyes timidly from Cara's face.

"Uh, sure, if you're up to it. I can replace the dressing, and the water isn't going to hurt anything. In fact, it would be good to keep the area clean and let the water run over the sutures.

Cara's eyes lingered a moment on Jake's face. "I'd appreciate it, thanks."

"Okay," Jake said, rubbing her hands together, "you'll find clean towels and everything you need in the cabinet in the bathroom off your room. Come out and have something to eat when you're done; you have to be hungry."

Cara watched Jake disappear through the archway, puzzled at the effect this woman had on her.

Cara stood in front of the mirror looking at the stitches on her side. *I could put a dressing on this myself if I could just reach—ouch! Okay, that's out! Well, I guess the good doctor can do her thing.*

She pondered the last forty-eight hours, especially the exasperating blonde doctor.

Curious...I wouldn't have bet two cents that I could spend an hour in the same room with the woman, let alone be sleeping in her bed. Well, not exactly her bed, not that the feisty doc doesn't rouse my curiosity. Hmm, methinks there is far more to the beautiful doctor than meets the eye.

A knock on the door followed by Jake's voice interrupted Cara's thoughts.

"You ready for a clean dressing?"

As ready as I'll ever be. Buttoning the even-large-for-her pajama top, Cara answered, "Sure, come in."

Jake struggled to hide the smile that threatened to develop into a full-fledged chuckle as she watched Cara roll up the extra long sleeves of the top that came to just above her knees. Incredible as it seemed, standing in her bathroom, smelling of apricot-peach scented body wash, half-naked, was the woman she had despised for the past two years. Her wet dark hair hung softly around her freshly scrubbed face. *She's so much...younger than I remember.*

Cara quizzed with a raised eyebrow, "Hmm...let me see...a *friend's* jammies, perhaps?"

"Uh, no sorry to disappoint, but they belonged to my dad," Jake responded with feigned sarcasm. A wicked smirk played across her face as she ordered, "Now, you can take it off so I can play doctor—and don't even think of telling me to turn around."

Bossy thing. So she thinks she has me with this one...well, let's just see about that, Doc. Challenged by the amused look on Jake's face, Cara leveled her eyes on her as she slowly unbuttoned the shirt and removed it. She stood facing Jake in all her naked glory, smugly taking in Jake's reaction.

Jake tried in vain not to let her glance travel down the body in front of her. *Ooh, she did this on purpose.* She gulped. *My god, she doesn't play fair!* Flustered and hoping Cara wouldn't notice her obviously crimson cheeks, she diverted her attention to the wound on Cara's side. She mustered her most professional demeanor to cover her unease.

"All right, let's get this cleaned and redressed."

The fun of getting one up on Jake set aside, Cara was suddenly conscious of the way Jake's fingers felt on her skin as she reapplied the dressing. They were gentle, reassuring, yet distracting in a way that disturbed her. She felt Jake tremble but was afraid to look at their reflections in the mirror, terrified at what she might see. And afraid that Jake might see through the façade, the staid detachment that had been her refuge.

"Okay, we're done." Jake's thoughts were in overdrive as she finished tending to Cara's wound. She weighed her combination of confusion and disbelief at standing in her bathroom with a naked Cara Vittore. More confusing still was her reaction to the sensation of Cara's supple skin on her fingertips and their being in the same breathing space. Strangely enough, she didn't want the feeling or the closeness to end.

"It looks good, should heal nicely if you take care and follow doctor's orders." Avoiding a repeat embarrassing scrutiny of Cara's body, Jake turned and stepped out of the bathroom.

"I fixed some sandwiches, come out and have something to eat...uh...when you finish dressing." Jake swore she heard a chalk-one-up-for-Cara chuckle as she headed toward the kitchen to retrieve the food.

A sudden flash of lightning filled the room, causing the lights to flicker momentarily. Seconds later, the still night split with the resounding crash of thunder. The monsoon storm, in full wrath, alternated between violent clashes in the sky and the steady battering of rain against the windows.

"That was a good one!" Cara exclaimed in appreciation of the sudden illumination.

"You wouldn't think so if we were out there," replied Jake as she pointed beyond the large picture windows.

"We were out there, remember?" Cara retorted good-naturedly. "I have the battle scars to prove it. You, my friend, even got to fly around the misty skies in a helicopter."

"Looking for you!" Jake said incredulously, trying to hold back the mirth that threatened to escape. "Are you always so annoying?"

"Yes, some people seem to think so! And I wasn't where you were looking—I was miles down the wash, hanging on to Stat for dear life."

The easy banter that now seemed to characterize their interaction ended when both fell into a quiet, reflective moment of stillness.

Jake reviewed the events of the past two days. They'd done it. They had beaten the odds and survived an arroyo flash flood. She glanced sideways at the sharp profile of the injured woman, impressed with Cara's easy banter and ability to minimize the harrowing experience. The shower seemed to have erased much of the tiredness from her face and body, but Jake knew the battered woman had to be uncomfortable. The bizarre combination of fire and steel that was Cara Vittore remained a mystery to Jake: the energy that pulsed beneath her unruffled surface; the pure pragmatism and intelligence that was offset by a raging passionate nature that could not quite be extinguished, despite being well constrained. And Jake was confounded as to how to remain unyielding to its force or how she could weave through the intricacies of this woman.

For Cara, everything hurt. Her arm hurt. Her back hurt. Even her hair hurt. She had been near physical exhaustion, struggling to save herself and Stat after being swept into the middle of the flash flood. Luckily, the horse had saved both of them, finding his footing and hauling them out of the arroyo to safety. Although she still felt the effects, her senses were keen. She casually studied the willowy woman setting food on the carved oaken coffee table. The lawyer was impressed by the balance of strength and beauty that emanated from this conflicting woman. Her gaze lingered on Jake's lovely face, the expressive hazel eyes, and the silky blonde hair tied loosely at the back of her neck. So well disciplined was Cara, so automatic had the reining-in of any impulse that threatened her become, that she was almost unaware of these feelings. Life had groomed her well. Yet now, she who had perfected the persona of remaining untouched by human weakness and emotion found herself fighting resolutely to ignore the suggestive images that filled her mind at the sight of Jake's long legs and slim, tanned hands.

"Do you need anything? Something to drink, maybe?" Jake asked.

"Do you have any wine?"

"It doesn't mix with the pain meds," Jake admonished.

"I didn't take any, but a glass of good wine would soothe the soul...and the aches."

Jake supposed a celebration of sorts was in order and walked to the small cabinet in the corner of the room. After a moment of deliberation, she held up the bottle of Merlot.

"I've been threatening to open this for a long while; now is as good a time as any."

Uncorking the bottle, she poured two glasses, then handed one to Cara.

"My father gave me this bottle of wine when I graduated from med school. I've been saving it for a special occasion."

Jake was struck by Cara's introspective appearance as she watched slender hands reach to touch the bottle. The silence that accompanied the sensual manner in which she held the wine bottle, coupled with the distance in Cara's eyes as she gazed at it and then to the contents of the glass swirling in the light, sparked an odd sense in Jake that she was intruding upon a intimate moment for Cara. Jake stepped back into the kitchen to get a snack of cheese and fruit to go with the wine, leaving Cara to her moment of reflection alone.

Cara recognized the all too familiar bottle of Cipriano Merlot. She had no idea that a single bottle still remained from the vintage of that year of disparate emotions. It was the year simple joys had flourished along with the grapes, the year of tumultuous sorrows when the innocence of youth had fled. Memories surged in like a tsunami—she couldn't have held them back if she had tried. That year, her grandfather had named her *padrone*, and the relic she held now was from the first bottling she had overseen, albeit still under his watchful eye since she had not yet completed her education. It had been the summer of the fastest car and the best wine, the year of sensual pleasures of adolescent freedom and awakening. She saw Stephen splashing in the blue-green waters of the Pacific, his face grinning with the love and admiration of a little brother who idolized his big sister and their best friend Maggie.

Cara's heart fluttered as she remembered how he never could disguise his feelings when he looked at Maggie. *I don't think he even tried,* she silently mused. Yellow paint flashed in her mind with the memory of the '79 Triumph TR7, of how she and Stephen had restored that little gem to mint condition. She couldn't suppress the outward smile as she recalled the "discussion" about the color. She had wanted black, but Stephen insisted that it should be the original yellow—something about how it reminded him of how a streak of lightning might look if it raced down the PCH. And then he had flashed her that idolizing, toothy grin while explaining ever so logically how cool he would be cruising Cabrillo Boulevard in the fastest car with the two prettiest girls in Santa Barbara, even if one was his big sister. As usual, Stephen had gotten his way with her.

Oh my, but we were just children. I was only nineteen, Maggie was seventeen, and Stephen was barely sixteen. It had been the summer of wild abandon. Never again would they enjoy such a time, these moments now locked away like fossils in amber. Oh, the countless mornings when the three of them threw only a halter on their horses and rode bareback, tearing headlong and carefree across the terraces. *Last one to the old oak has to brush down the horses! And sweep out the stalls!* Stephen's laughter rang clear in her mind. She could see his inky black hair billowing in the wind as they raced toward the edge of the vineyard. How many times had she let him win? And the nights hurtling down the PCH, moonlight gleaming like a white ribbon on the ocean, in the little yellow streak of lightning that zipped down the highway.

Cara's mind raced to the morning she had left for Harvard. She saw again the hint of a tear on Stephen's cheeks as he promised to take care of Grandfather until she returned. She knew he was being brave for her sake, knew how the boy would miss her. She knew too, she would never again see the love and admiration in his eyes, knew how his heart would break, if he found out that Maggie had spent the night in her bed. *My god, little brother, I am so sorry.*

Cara wasn't aware of Jake or anything else—except the flood of memories the year on the wine bottle evoked—until—

"What do you think?" Jake asked, watching Cara swirl the wine in her glass. "A good year?"

She sensed Cara's thoughts were an unwelcome foray into something that obviously troubled her. "My dad was the connoisseur, and he valued this bottle. He said it was, hmm...let me see...it was the 'judicious blending of the noble, heady Cabernet Sauvignon and lush, velvety Merlot that tamed the tannic red.'"

"Your father was right," Cara whispered, her mind wandering to the day she had approached her grandfather with her idea to do just that. He had listened tacitly. When she was finished, he smiled, "You are my choice for *padrone, cara mia*. The grapes, they love you. You will nurture them, create your destiny. It is your legacy."

"Your father knew his wine."

Jake smiled, reaching back into the wine cabinet to produce another aged bottle of red that she handed to Cara. "Well, I guess he did at that."

Looking at the private label, Cara questioned, "This wine was made here, in Santa Cruz County?"

"Yes. When my dad retired from the FBI, he bought a partner's interest in a small vineyard owned by Matt's father. He took full responsibility for the grapes and wine after Matt's father died. Matt and Sandro were too young to shoulder the responsibility themselves. Maria, Matt's mother, you met her at the café, hadn't been involved in the making of the wine—too busy raising two boys and running the café."

"Sandro? Is that the same guy who is with the Mexican police?"

Jake looked at Cara quizzically. "You've met Sandro?"

"No, Matt was talking to him on the phone in Maria's the day I got here. He lived with Matt's family?"

"Yes, Maria raised Sandro. We all grew up together, went to the same schools here in Nogales. Sandro went back across the border to live and work with the Mexican police after he and Matt came home from the service."

Cara's gaze went from the bottle of wine back to Jake. "Where is your father now?"

Jake's eyes clouded with deep sorrow. "Dead. He was murdered."

"Murdered? Wait, Jack Biscayne, two years ago. Wasn't he killed investigating the Rivera drug cartel? I remember reading about that case. It was never solved, was it?"

Jake held in the tears she felt stinging her eyes. "No, it's still open with no arrests and no leads. He spent thirty years with the FBI and came out of retirement as a consultant. He was always so aware, so careful. It's still hard for me to believe someone got close enough to kill him without a struggle."

Cara felt guilty. She had been so self-absorbed that she hadn't recognized Jake had her own story, her own grief. Steadying her gaze on Jake's moist hazel eyes, she reached over and held her hand. "I'm sorry, I know it is never easy to lose someone you love, let alone for them to be taken so brutally."

Two years ago, that was about the time of the Pendleton trial! No wonder she missed that loophole in the evidence.

Cara's touch conveyed more than the warmth of her skin. The deliberate expressiveness within that simple gesture traveled throughout Jake's body like ripples on a lake when a pebble is dropped in. She lifted her face to Cara's and returned a look of acknowledgment into caring, brown eyes. In that moment, something passed between them—the mutual recognition of kindred souls burdened by loss and pain.

No, Cara, it isn't, especially when you lose the two most important people in your world within weeks of each other, both murdered.

Jake barely nodded and squeezed her fingers around Cara's. The two women sat in comfortable silence watching the monsoon light up the Arizona sky until Jake sensed the extent of Cara's fatigue. "Hey there, I think you could use another good night's rest, don't you?"

Cara's voice belied the weariness deep in her bones. "I need to call my office, I usually check in everyday when I'm gone. They'll be wondering what happened to me..."

"Tomorrow. You can call then, and no, they won't be worried. I called your office and talked to Lara. She said that Mark is aware of the situation and insisted that you take some R and R to recover. Oh, before I forget, he said to remind you, if you're up to it, about the arrival of the new associate at the end of next week. Now," pulling Cara up from the sofa, "doctor's orders, one good night's sleep."

"You're a bossy thing. Do I have anything to say about...anything?"

"Nope, might as well accept it."

Crossing her arms across her chest, Cara offered a bargain. "Say, if I go quietly, how about showing me around tomorrow? I'd like to see your ranch and the vineyards."

"A bit of blackmail here?" Jake asked with a quiet chuckle, pointing to the guestroom. "We'll see, now to bed with you."

Chapter Six

L ying awake, Cara looked around the spacious stucco-walled room. Subtle shades of aged parchment and sand were enhanced by decorative drapings of hand-woven Mexican rugs. Splashes of color from similar rugs adorned the cool Saltillo tile floor as well. The rustic black walnut furniture absorbed soft light cast from twin wrought iron lamps. A Spanish guitar leaned against a beautifully carved old walnut chest that graced the foot of a four-poster bed.

Cara pulled the quilt up and gazed out the glass doors to a natural garden of upland desert plants. Stirred by the rhythm of the storm, she threw back the covers and reached for the guitar. Running her long fingers over the strings, she noticed the exquisite artistry of the abalone and mother-of-pearl inlays on the neck and the intricate mosaic rosette that circled above the pick guard. Resting against the pillows, she cradled the instrument in her arms. The wine, the emotions, all of it was inextricably connected in her mind with the year she had left the vineyards for college. She inhaled deeply as her fingers eased up the neck of the guitar. The chords of a song permeated the room, and the memories came back to her.

The sleek curves of the guitar under her fingertips drew her mind to the day she had walked into the Keltic Knot, a small pub just off campus, looking for a job. The proprietor, Liam Quinn, had been her mother's dearest friend. And not surprisingly, he had been Vittore Cipriano's fiercest rival, both men vying for the hand of the woman who had become Cara's mother. Cara was the spitting image of her mother Daire, whom Liam never stopped loving even after she and Cara's father were killed in an auto accident just after Stephen's birth.

It had been fifteen years since he'd seen a child of Daire's, since the day of the funeral. Liam stretched his back, then tiredly scrubbed his stubbled face with both hands.

"How many more is there, Kenzie girl? There must be one out of the bunch that can carry an Irish tune," he yelled in a thick Irish brogue. "If not, run the lot of 'em out of here."

"This is the last one, and don't be a-yellin' at me, Liam Quinn," McKenzie, the strawberry-blonde bartender, snapped back. She had been eyeing the compellingly beautiful, dark-eyed woman since her arrival to interview for the job of bartender, waiter, and when necessary, songster.

"Go on, give it a go," McKenzie urged. "Can ya play something of the Irish?"

Cara picked up her guitar and crossed the dance floor to the stool in the middle of the small stage. Sitting with one foot on a rung of the stool and one planted solidly on the floor, she began to strum the guitar and sing.

As the chords of the old Irish melody "Deora Ar Mo Chroí (Tears On My Heart)" filled the room, Liam's naturally red face dulled to an ashen grey. He listened and lifted his eyes from the stack of invoices and other papers he was checking. It was as if he were seeing his beloved Daire reaching from the grave to touch his lonely soul one more time.

He felt the tears on his own heart with each line the young woman sang. The song had been her favorite; Liam listened unabashed with tears in his eyes. Tears for his lost love. He looked upon the very image of his Daire as he took in the features of the singer.

"Be here tonight at eight and bring your instrument there with ya." And with a wistful tone he asked, "What's yer name, girl?"

Cara laid the guitar across her lap and cocked her head the same way her mother always had. "Cara, sir, Cara Vittore Cipriano."

With a silent nod of acceptance, the large Irishman retreated to his office and into his memories.

The mellow chords of a guitar blended with the peaceful night sounds and nudged Jake from a light sleep. Slipping from under the covers, she crossed the room to the veranda door to listen. The music came from the guestroom that faced her bedroom across a shared courtyard. Realizing it was Cara playing, she was astounded by yet another aspect of this mystifying woman. *She constantly contradicts everything I believed about her.* Jake's image of the cold, blasé attorney was fading. In its place, a genuine liking for the surprisingly compassionate woman was growing. Climbing into her bed, she gathered a pillow to her chest and drifted back to sleep, listening to the soothing harmony of the guitar accompanied by the intermittent howl of a nearby coyote.

Jake woke to the smell of coffee and the light of dawn filtering through her window. Lying with her eyes closed, she allowed the beckoning aroma and the stirring sounds of morning coming alive again to ease her aching body into the day. Suddenly, her eyes flew open.

"Coffee! It's too early for Juanita! She's up making coffee?"

After a quick shower, Jake hurried into a pair of jeans and a white T-shirt. She followed the tantalizing scent down the hall to the kitchen where she found Cara leisurely leaning against the counter with a steaming cup of coffee in her hands looking out the window.

"I hope you don't mind." Cara filled a cup for Jake and motioned for her to sit at the table. "I thought you might need some coffee."

Jake's eyes were transfixed on the sight before her, this woman, this "top gun" lawyer in her bare feet and an old shirt with a dish towel tucked in the waist of some faded old jeans that had belonged to Jake's dad. *And fixing breakfast, no less!* Trying to get past her amazement, Jake remembered to ask, "Um, how are you feeling, your ribs sore?"

"I won't deny it, I am a bit stiff. But the more I move around the more it loosens up. I took some ibuprofen I found in your medicine cabinet. Come on, let's eat, then you can show me your ranch."

The secluded ranch lay nestled in the foothills of the high desert grasslands between the majestic Santa Ritas and the arresting red Patagonia Mountains. Biscayne Hacienda, built by her grandfather in the early 1900s, was the quintessential portrait of old-world Mexico's charm and warmth. Sweeping grasslands, dotted with yucca, horses, and cattle, undulated lazily up toward the high peaks. She had thinned out her herd of horses so much over the past few years that to call herself a rancher anymore was pushing it. Neighboring spreads, however, still epitomized the grand idea of what it meant to be an Arizona rancher.

Sitting on the veranda surrounded by towering cottonwoods, Cara watched a herd of quarter horses lazily pasturing on green grass. When they had toured the wine country of Sonoita and Elgin earlier, she was impressed with the beauty of the area. She was even more surprised to learn that the red soil, very nearly identical to that of Burgundy, France, produced exceptional quality wine grapes of several varieties, including Cabernet Sauvignon, Merlot, Syrah,

Chardonnay, Sauvignon Blanc, and Sangiovese. Jake came through the veranda door with two glasses of a Merlot they'd purchased at one of the vineyards they had stopped at earlier.

It had been a long day, and the two women sat contentedly sipping wine and discussing the merits of the grape as the Arizona sunset painted the horizon the color of amethyst—spectacular rose and deep purple. Jake fondly recalled the many times when she and her father sat at this very time of evening watching the sun set as they debated the virtue of one of the vintages aging in oak barrels in the cool natural earth caves of the winery.

Cara tilted her glass, watching the tears drip down the inside. "I like it. Crisp finish with a surprisingly good balance. There's potential—another two years of proper aging, and this will be a keeper."

Jake avidly listened to the detailed attributes of the young vintage. Sparkling in Cara's eyes was an enthusiasm that suffused her entire body as if she were alive with a sensual animation. Jake's attention soon fell on Cara's exquisite hands. Long fingers caressed the smooth wineglass, mesmerizing Jake with each evocative stroke of a lone index finger moving sensuously across the rim.

"What's your opinion, Jake? Jake, what do you think?"

Jake shook her head, refocusing her attention on Cara's voice. She tried to contain her embarrassment as she stammered, "Oh, uh, yes I agree," feeling a bit awkward, wondering what to say and if Cara noticed the rosy flush on her cheeks that surely rivaled the setting sun. "You know your wine."

Cara knew the only time she felt alive was when she was immersed in the vineyards and the smell of the earth and the wine-soaked oaken aging caskets. At that moment, looking into Jake's eyes, she felt the same excitement she always felt standing on the hill with the ocean to her back while her eyes lovingly surveyed row upon row of ripening grapes. An irresistible need to reach out to feel the comfort of this woman overwhelmed her as brown eyes met and held hazel ones. Jake shifted in her chair and leaned toward Cara. They were close enough to feel the breath of the other when the telephone rang, interrupting the unanticipated moment.

Flustered, Jake jumped up and went inside to answer the phone.

"Hello...yes, she's here, just a moment." Setting the phone down on the table, she walked back out on the veranda. "It's for you."

The pounding of her heart was louder than the bits of conversation heard through the open door. With hands and thoughts shaky, she fought to compose herself.

What was I thinking! What if I had...get a grip here. You invite, no, insist this woman stay here after nearly getting her killed, then you let your thoughts run rampant!

Not wanting to explore the reason for her actions and thoughts toward Cara, Jake started clearing away the wineglasses as she listened to Cara's one-sided conversation.

"Mark, can you slow down enough to tell me why you're calling this late? I see, when did they release him? Good...good, yes, I'll be in the office early tomorrow. Yes...oh, and Mark, what happened to those 'few days of R and R' I deserved?"

Cara hung up the phone, but her mind was not on what Mark had just told her. Instead, she held the image of what had almost transpired between her and Jake. The scene faded as reality reminded her that she would be leaving tomorrow. Jake came through the door, wineglasses in hand, and stopped as Cara's questioning brown eyes searched her face. Cara reached up to touch Jake's cheek just as the phone rang again.

Breaking eye contact, Jake picked up the receiver.

"Hello." Jake paused as she listened. "When, Matt?" She ran a hand through her hair as she processed what she was hearing. "I guess the Sierra Vista brig is a pretty good alibi, don't you? I never believed he was our guy." A moment passed. "Yes, I'll tell her, she's here. You sound tired, Matt, better get some rest. We have a killer to find."

Turning to find Cara across the room looking out the window, Jake relayed Matt's message in her best attempt at a professional voice.

"You know your client was released to the MPs from Sierra Vista? Seems he'd been missing roll call and was serving a week in the brig. He wasn't released until the day after we found the last girl. The condition of the body made in difficult to pinpoint the exact time of death, but I do know she could not have been there a whole week."

"That's what Chase was calling to tell me. He got a call from some highly placed suits who are watching this case telling us we would not be needed anymore. Seems they knew before the authorities here did."

Fortifying her emotions, Jake reasoned, "Yes, with all the political implications of the North American Free Trade Agreement on the table, allowing Mexican trucks to go beyond the twenty-mile commercial limit and U.S. trucks into the Mexican interior, many influential concerns don't want the bad press. Hence, a serial killer using the border as his hunting grounds will not be acceptable."

The intensity of the moment on the veranda had been eclipsed by the interruptions. Jake's quiet voice broke the silence that had descended like a cloud.

"If you have to drive back to Tucson early in the morning, you better get some sleep."

Cara found only an implacable expression when she looked at Jake. Knowing further conversation was futile, she mutely nodded her head in assent as Jake walked toward her room without looking back.

"Good night, Cara."

Peering intently out the window into the shadows, Cara searched for a rationalization that would ease her agitated thoughts. She furrowed her brow and gave herself a plausible answer for the last ten minutes.

We've been through an emotional few days. It isn't unusual for people to get caught up in that intensity, to be drawn to each other. It happens in these situations. More than likely, I read more into it than there was, assuming it was more than just friendship offered. Was she going to kiss me? A cold reality collided with Cara's senses.

Shimmering gently, the western sun sank into the peaceful haze. It reflected off the copper-domed building that housed Cara's office. Nearby buildings that normally went unnoticed suddenly came out of their obscurity, delicately bathed in subtle, dusky colors. It was one of those evenings when the last cloud lost its sharp cranberry edge and melted into the city. From above, the dome resembled some remarkable jewel, nestled between the shaded depths of undulating mountains.

Languishing twilight shadows danced their ephemeral, crimson-tinted dapplings through Cara's top-floor office. The gloaming. She marveled at this evanescent time between dark and light when the hustle of Tucson slowed. The gloaming was her time for contemplating the ending of the day's long work. Transported into its magical quietness and mystery, she could put events into perspective and ready herself for the next day. But that night was different somehow. The gloaming draped over her like a fiery cape of hunger. Intertwining dark and light etched a loneliness in the pit of her stomach that mimicked the feeling in her heart—as it had every evening since she had left the ranch at Rio Rico. As the lonesome shadows deepened with the fading light, Cara realized the depth of her aloneness. She hadn't given much thought to how isolated life had become, not until she met the irresistible, feisty doctor.

The sudden intrusion of Mark Chase sticking his head through the open door of the office pulled her back from her contemplations.

"Hey, you've been burning the midnight oil every night since you got back. Why don't you give it a break and come have a drink with us?"

She lifted a questioning eyebrow. "Us?"

"I'm meeting the new associate to personally deliver a contract that we hope will be signed by tomorrow...and to kiss up a bit. We've sweetened the offer for this one, so be on your best behavior at tomorrow's welcoming meeting." He gave Cara a dubious look. "Okay?"

Pausing to scrutinize Cara from top to bottom, his expression softened as he peered over the top of his glasses and spoke in earnest. "Shit, you look terrible. You need to relax, Cara. You're driving yourself too hard. Pack it in. And I won't take no for an answer. Whatever you're chasing can wait until tomorrow."

"Mark I really need to finish this tonight, I—"

Cara sat under Mark's stern gaze as he interrupted, determination clear in his voice. "You have two choices here. One, we go get something to eat and deliver these papers to our new hopeful. Or two, you get the hell out of here and go home. Your choice."

Looking wearily at Mark and knowing it would be futile to argue, Cara reluctantly yielded, but with stipulations of her own. With all the aloofness of a lawyer determined to bluff a jury, she countered the options.

"I'll take your offer, Counselor, if you buy me a burger on the way and if it's a one-drink limit and if we go over the Taylor deposition. It's a package deal, take it or leave it."

"Oh, you're good, trying to play the negotiator with me. But no shop talk for you tonight."

"We'll see," Cara said confidently.

"Tomorrow we'll catch up. Finish up and meet me downstairs in fifteen minutes. You can follow me to the Radisson."

Cara nodded her agreement, and Mark dashed off. She turned her attention to the photos of the murdered girl that she never had reviewed the day of the flash flood or during her recuperation at Jake's ranch. The rage-inspired butchery that took the life of this girl and her unborn child appalled her. This slaughter, this torture...it was beyond all human reason.

Their hands are tied. This animal preys on the vulnerable, then slinks back to goddamned Mexico. How many more are there? How many more will there be? How long has he been doing this? And how do you go back and forth across the line with no hint of suspicion? Ah, your first mistake, muchacho. *Never leave me with a question I can find an answer for. Because I will find it.*

An overwhelming anger seethed within her, fueling her desire to stop this atrocity to the human race. She reached to touch a computer composite of the girl.

They'll never catch your killer, not as long as their jurisdictional powers don't carry over the line into Mexico. There must be a way!

Nursing her second particularly strong margarita, Cara finally began to relax. It seemed Mark had been gone especially long delivering the contract papers to the new associate. Outside, the temperature was still over a hundred degrees, so the respite of the cool Saguaro Lounge was relaxingly welcome, and soon her eyes closed as thoughts of a certain hazel-eyed doctor drifted in.

I would have liked to spend more time with her. I like her smile and spirited way when she's angry. Oh, and those eyes, they show all her emotion. She intrigues me, her quietness and compassion, the softness. Matt's in love with her, a blind man could see that! Are they lovers? Does she belong to him? Geez, Cara, get a grip here, there's no way possible she could be interested in you. But...she is something.

Glancing at her watch, Cara grumbled to herself. *So much for getting the price of a burger out of Mark.* It was getting late, and her empty stomach protested at not being fed well over the past week. She drained the last of the margarita, threw a bill on the bar for her tab, and bent to gather up her briefcase. A tap on her shoulder accompanied by the familiar honeyed tones of a gentle Irish brogue made her heart flutter.

"Can ya buy an Irish lass a pint, love?" Turning toward the voice, Cara found herself looking into the vivid green eyes of McKenzie Quinn, Liam's daughter. And her lover throughout her college years.

Brilliant green eyes of the petite woman wandered affectionately over Cara, who blinked in disbelief. "Kenzie? What? Where did...what are you doing here?"

McKenzie edged forward. "Is that the only welcome a girl would be gettin', Cara Cipriano?" Putting her arms around the taller woman's waist and pulling her into an embrace, McKenzie's voice dropped to a secretive whisper. "How about a bit of a hug here?"

As the two embraced, McKenzie couldn't stop the hitch in her breath and the shiver that traveled down her spine at the sensation of having this woman in her arms again. She pressed her lips to Cara's ear. "It's been too long, I've missed you."

Mark Chase exited the men's room and headed toward the bar, slowing mid-stride when he saw the two embracing women.

That's curious, Cara didn't say she knew Quinn, or for that matter the other way around. He cleared his voice to announce his presence. "Uh, I didn't know you two knew each other?"

Cara was speechless. McKenzie smiled, her eyes never leaving Cara.

"I didn't make the connection at first. The name Vittore threw me. You never used it at Harvard, just Cipriano." Holding tight to Cara's hand as the memories returned, McKenzie added, "But a most welcome surprise it is."

McKenzie Quinn was waiting at the pub for her lover to arrive. The day before had been their last day at law school, and Cara was leaving for her home in California on that June morning to attend her younger brother Stephen's wedding. They promised to make every effort to see each other, but a cold ache rested balefully in her heart. She had loved this woman from the first moment she sat on that stool in her father's pub, brown eyes full of life and emotion, playing her guitar and singing as sweet as the Emerald Isle itself. She would never forget the shock on Cara's face when she found out she was the law student assigned as her mentor.

"What's the matter, yank? Guess ya thought I was only good for pulling pints, mopping up, and serving drunks, now didn't ya?" McKenzie teased as she sat the chairs down on the freshly mopped pub floor. "My grandmother always said, 'don't be judging a book by its cover, Kenzie girl, looks and impressions can be deceivin' ya for certain.' She was a firm believer that a person made her own way, no matter what her station in life."

Cara's mouth still hung open even as McKenzie's eyes twinkled above her broad, cat-ate-the-mouse grin.

"Besides, we all need shakin' up a bit now and then—don't we? Better close that mouth of yours or you'll be a-catchin' flies."

Chapter Seven

"Ready for some fun?" Kalani asked in an amused voice from her desk across the room.

"What?" Jake was a little baffled at the question.

"Fun, you do remember the concept, don't you?"

"Yes."

"Are you sure?"

Jake pressed her thumbs into fatigued eyes that had been fighting the urge to sleep. *Death by insomnia,* she thought. "What have you done now?" she asked sleepily. Her distress was superseded only by Kalani's delight.

"Dr. Raynard called this morning," she revealed.

Jake fell back against her chair, moaning up at the stuccoed ceiling.

"Sorry, this is the first chance I've had to tell you. He wanted to make sure you were attending his lectures in Tucson this weekend and said to tell you he took the liberty of reserving a seat for you."

Jake regarded her assistant careful before speaking. "No, I can't go. I have too much work here."

Easing from behind her desk, Kalani quietly walked over to where Jake was sitting and perched on the edge of her desk. Her eyes were gleaming. "He said he would not take no for an answer. And frankly, neither will I."

"I'm not going, Kalani. End of story." Jake craned her neck around at her assistant. "And just who made you the fun boss?"

Taking a more serious tone, Kalani leaned forward, gently squeezing a hand into Jake's shoulder. "Jake. It'll do you good to get away for a couple of days. The work will be taken care of, you know that. Besides, I already made your reservation at the Radisson. King Suite with a great view and all the room service you can handle."

Seeing no response, Kalani removed her hand and continued on another tack. She was not above doing a shakedown on Jake.

"There's something else. I have an ulterior motive for getting you out of town and off the job. I would like to take the two days off you'll be gone, if that's all right. I haven't been spending as much time with Teresa as I should. It's just that we have been so busy working on the Jane Doe cases I forget a nine-year-old needs her mother. So we're going to spend some quality time together and do the mother-daughter thing, shop for school clothes, take in a movie, maybe even indulge in a greasy, artery-clogging hamburger or two. She's already planning the weekend. You don't want to disappoint a nine-year-old, do you, Jake? Hello? Assistant to boss lady..."

The steady rhythm of a pencil eraser thrummed in time to Jake's thoughts. Paperwork unfinished, distractions from work, guilt about her lack of sensitivity to Kalani's personal life. All week she'd had trouble focusing, unsuccessful in pushing thoughts of a tall, enigmatic Cara Vittore from her mind. And she'd never even thought about the upcoming forensic symposium. Now Kalani's less than subtle reminder: life's simplicity in the eyes of a child. Suddenly, the reality check sank in and she smiled wistfully at her assistant, knowing she'd been steamrolled and that she needed it.

Jake smiled at the cagey Kalani. "Dr. Raynard, you're right, he is just what I need. Thank you for taking care of the reservation, and you do not need to ask. Of course you can have the time off. I know you've been working around the clock on these cases. I'm sorry your time with Teresa has suffered."

"No more than you, Jake. I know you slept on the couch here again last night, and the clothes you have on are the same ones you had on yesterday."

"It's here, I can feel it. It's mocking us, daring us to find it and we will, Kalani, we will." Jake wearily ran a hand through her blonde hair, apologetically leveling tired hazel eyes on her friend. "I'm sorry. I haven't been much of a friend lately, have I? I've been insensitive to your needs at home and totally inconsiderate of your social life." Jake mockingly raised both hands and laughed. "Oh! Forget I said that. Neither one of us knows the meaning of a social life! You're right, Kalani, the long weekend will give us both a better perspective."

Kalani studied the earnest face of the woman she considered her best friend. Jake was family. "Is everything all right, Jake? You haven't seemed yourself these past few days, well, since the narrow escape from the flash flood." Casting a inquisitive glance toward Jake, she pressed further. "Uh...how is Vittore doing, have you, uh, heard from her?"

Jake blushed slightly and shrugged, feigning interest in the untouched paper work in front of her to cover her self-consciousness. "Go home, woman, it's late."

She was rewarded with a sparkling smile. "Thanks, Jake. You should take your own advice and go home."

"Go!" Jake boomed in a hearty voice, happy to know that she'd put that smile there.

"I'm going, I'm going!"

Driving all thoughts but work from her mind, Jake was resigned to clear her desk before leaving to pack for the long weekend in Tucson. *I do need a break*, she thought. *Oh,*

Matt. I can't deal with you now either. Her thoughts roamed elsewhere, toying with the idea of calling Cara while she was in Tucson. *I could invite her for lunch. What would I say? I'll be in Tucson, do you want to go out for lunch? Why am I so nervous about inviting a friend to lunch? We did become friends...didn't we? And what was the night before she left for Tucson all about? Be honest, Jake, you didn't want her to leave. I would like to see her or at least call to ask how she is doing.*

"Damn, it's bad enough she was the bane of my existence for the past two years. Okay, so it was an unjustified torment. Now I actually miss her!" Jake turned back to her work. "Doesn't matter anyway. She's probably busy."

Matt Peyson had been having an all-around bad day. One of his rookie agents had shot a cow under what appeared to be dubious circumstances. *Damn rookie doesn't know a four-legged animal from a two-legged one!* His foreman at the vineyard had quit a few days ago, delaying a small order of wine that should have already been shipped. He was drowning in the bureaucracy of processing a vanload of illegals captured crossing the border near Patagonia, some he was getting to know on a first name basis. A civilian vigilante group over in Sierra Vista continued to wreck havoc, playing self-appointed Border Patrol agents with their satellite up-loads to the Internet. And Jake, well, Jake grew increasingly distant with each passing day. *Come to think of it,* he decided, *the past few weeks have been downright lousy.* Now he was pacing the kitchen floor in his mother's café, waiting to drive her home, as she busied herself with the dough for the morning sweet breads. It was past closing time, and he grappled to contain his growing irritation.

"Mama, it's darn near time to come back here; it's late, let's go."

"Watch your tone with me. Last time I looked, I was an adult and capable of getting myself home, thank you."

"You know I worry, especially now with these unsolved murders on our hands. I'll feel better if I know you're home safe and sound," Matt grumbled contritely.

Maria studied the rugged, handsome face of her son. "You've been irritable, what's bothering you?"

Drawing in a deep breath and letting it ease out to temper his edginess, he spoke as humbly as he could. "Nothing, Mama. Just work is all."

"Uh-huh, and Jake doesn't have a thing in the world to do with it, *mi hijo*?"

His first instinct was to deny his mother's presumption, but knowing he could never hide anything from her, he shrugged. "I have loved her as long as my memory of life is, Mama. I thought I'd lost her to Sam when they got engaged. Then the accident when he was killed, and she came home so lost and hurt only to have to face her dad's murder. I just wanted to take the hurt and pain away. I know she needed time, but for a while it seemed we were getting close again. I thought we had a chance, but she holes up in that cocoon she hides in."

"Don't pressure her, son. If it is meant to be, it will happen."

"I know, Mama. I'm not complaining, it's just that she seems so preoccupied, so restless lately." A sad, faraway look dulled Matt's blue eyes. "I will wait for her as long as it takes. Whatever time she needs."

"They have been working night and day on these terrible murders too, Matt. It can't be easy, dealing with the dead every day. You know she is called *La Mujer de la Muerte*."

"The Lady of the Dead. I know, Mama."

"She doesn't even have time to stop in the morning for coffee and when she does, it's because she has worked all night and is too tired to drive home. She needs to take a day or so off."

"Well, when I stopped in at her office today, Kalani told me Jake was going to Tucson tomorrow for the weekend. Maybe when she gets back you could fix up those tamales she likes?"

"You bring her home, and I will put some meat on her bones, *mi hijo*. Go tell her to have a good time in Tucson. She's in her office; her car is still in her parking space out back. By the time you get back, I'll be ready to go home." Shooing him toward the door, she ordered, "Now go."

Maria watched the emotions on her son's face. Even when he was a child, the thoughts behind those clear blue eyes were always easy for her to read.

Clearing his throat, he headed for the door. "I think I will. Could see if she needs anything done at the ranch while she's gone. And I should tell her that order of wine we were shipping to Santa Fe will be delayed a week or so. She still owns the third her dad left her." He brushed the flour gently off his mother's cheek. "Finish up, Mama, you look tired. I'll be right back to take you home."

Maria watched Matt cut across the back parking lot to Jake's office. A sadness squeezed her heart. *You love her so much, but will she break your heart?*

Jake held her face in her hands, balancing herself with her elbows on the counter as she stood by the coffeepot. She was exhausted. Her hair was in complete disarray, and her wrinkled lab coat hung loosely over her body. Stretching, then straightening up enough to take her coffee mug in her hand, she inhaled the strong aroma of the spicy Guatemala and took a sip.

God, this is strong enough to raise the dead, but that's what I feel like.

Sighing and taking another drink of the strong coffee to ward off sleep, she shook her head but still couldn't stifle the yawn. *Kalani's right, I need a break...and some sleep.* Since the discovery of the last body and her soul-searching encounter with Cara, sleep had eluded her as she chased the shadows of her mind across her bedroom wall. *Why have I been thinking about Sam and the accident more lately?*

She stared into the cup, transfixed by the steaming blackness that seemed to elicit the memories of those dark days after Sam, her fiancé, was killed in her car in a fiery explosion that was meant for her. He had grabbed her keys by mistake and stomped out of their apartment that day. The argument they'd had was the worst so far. They were both angry, and he was late for a briefing on a major drug bust his team had been working on for over a year. Instead of going back in to get his own keys, he had jumped into Jake's Jeep. The explosion killed five others who were unlucky enough to be on the street that day, including two of their neighbors who were waiting in front of the apartment for the bus.

In Jake's mind, it was like yesterday. The blast tore out the windows of the building and bounced cars around as if they were toys. It looked like a war zone. Jake had been knocked off her feet, stunned. When she managed to get outside, the horror she saw was unreal. Her eyes traveled to the hole where the Jeep used to be, then to the bloody body parts strewn across the lawn. She remembered thinking before everything went black that they didn't belong there, how oddly out of place they seemed.

Three days later, she had woken up in the hospital in a panic. A respirator, assisting her scorched and edematous lungs with each breath, hissed beside her. Bandages concealed and protected her face. Gauze-wrapped hands burned with excruciating pain when she tried to bend her fingers. Later she learned that she had literally torn the door off a van that was engulfed in flames to get to a mother and her child. The child had died; the mother clung to life for several days until she learned of her child's death. Then she had just given up and died. Jake's body had healed, and over time, the scars had faded. But the wound in her heart and soul remained.

Lost in her memories and mesmerized by the contents of her cup, she jumped when a knock splintered the silence.

"Who can that be this hour?" she groaned, although she suspected it was Matt. He often stopped in to check on her when she worked late. She grumbled aloud and dragged herself to the outer office door.

An exhausted breath escaped her lips when she saw Matt standing just outside the entry. She attempted to fortify herself, pulling back her tangled sandy hair, holding it in a ponytail.

"Good God, I look like hell. Not that it matters anyway," she said under her breath and let go of her hair. "Hi, Matt. What brings you by so late?"

"May I come in?" he asked, not making eye contact but surveying her quietly.

"I'm a mess, but sure, come on in." She moved aside, allowing him into her office.

As Jake closed the door, she watched him walk to the chair by her desk, as he always did, calmly waiting as she closed the door. *He is so predictable, so dependable,* she thought to herself. *Any woman would be lucky to have him.*

"Can I get you a coffee?" Jake asked, stepping back over to her cup.

Matt looked up, expressionless. "Sure. Black would be fine," he replied, scrutinizing her every move.

She got a mug from the cabinet and filled it. When she turned back around, she was very aware that he was watching her.

I can't do this tonight, she thought tiredly and walked back to her desk, handing Matt the mug.

Briefly, his fingers caressed hers as he took it from her, still watching her. She could feel his eyes on her body. Matt looked into her eyes again, now with visible desire, and took a slow sip of his coffee; he placed the mug on the desk and rubbed his chin, a habit he had when he was stressed.

"So what are you doing here, Matt?" she asked distractedly.

"Thought I would stop in to see if you needed anything done out at the ranch while you're gone. And for a cup of coffee."

She arched an eyebrow at him.

"That is to say, I wanted some coffee with you," he corrected himself, picking up his mug for another sip.

She waited for Matt to tell her what was on his mind as she leaned against her desk.

He put the coffee down. His face took on a more serious expression as he walked to within inches of her. She held her position leaning against the desk as he moved in a little closer, too close. Jake swallowed hard and closed her eyes, trying to compose herself. *Not this...not tonight, Matt*, she pleaded in her mind. She had no strength to deal with it all. She opened her eyes again to find he had moved in closer, almost touching his lips to hers, but it was the touch of his hand to hers that startled her.

"Please, Matt, stop," she begged.

"Why?" he asked, moving in to brush his lips against hers.

"Because, we've been over this before. Isn't that enough? We agreed to give it some time, and I'm just too tired right now," she said and stepped away.

"Jake," he whispered, pulling her firmly against him. "Don't turn away from me."

Tears welled up in her eyes. *I can't,* she repeated in her mind as warm brown eyes flashed before her instead of blue. He looked passionately into her eyes, holding her by the shoulders as he moved in to touch his lips to hers. She reached one hand out to caress his cheek.

"I miss you so much, Jake. I lo—"

She pressed a finger to his lips to stop him. "Go home, Matt. Please."

"So glad I caught you two." Sandro's voice interrupted them, filling the room.

"Christ, Sandro! Why don't you knock before you scare the hell out of somebody!" Matt barked.

Sandro could feel the tension between his two closest friends. He laughed and started to ramble on about going to a club across the line. "It is a matter of great urgency, Mateo, that we get you and this beautiful woman out for some fun tonight."

"Sorry, Sandy. I've got an early trip in the morning, and I don't intend to start it with a hangover and no sleep," Jake informed him.

"Jake's got a conference in Tucson this weekend," Matt explained. "After I get Mama home, we were just going to have a quiet dinner."

Jake shot Matt a look that told him he had overstepped the line.

"I ran into Katarina again this afternoon." Sandro started up again, now more animated. Just the four of us...old times, *compañero*."

Jake wasn't fully listening and began to fall back into thoughts of Cara and Tucson when Sandro slipped his hand into hers and tilted her chin up with the other to look into her eyes.

"It's been a long time, Jacquelyn. Come, we will have fun, yes, just as always."

"Oh, it's tempting, but no, my friend." Jake exhaled and began to push him toward the door.

Sandro held up. "What do you mean *no*? The night, she is young and just waiting to be enjoyed." He smiled.

Matt could see Jake had reached her limit with both of them. Stepping in, he hurried Sandro out the door. "Come on, *amigo,* we will paint the town until dawn and drink the well dry—just as soon as I get Mama home."

Jake closed the door after them. *Thank God!* she said to herself and threw up her hands, running them through her hair. "I need to get out of here before I explode. The work can wait."

Standing before the full-length mirror in her suite at the Radisson, Jake surveyed her reflection. She had chosen to go comfortable and casual for Dr. Raynard's lecture that afternoon, allowing her sun-streaked hair to hang loosely on her shoulders. After one last look of approval at her light grey summer-weight slacks, teal silk long-sleeved blouse complimented by Navajo silver earrings and necklace, she slipped on a pair of sandals, tucked the large manila envelope under one arm, and headed down to the conference room.

Dr. Philip Raynard was one of the leading forensic scientists in the country, and as one of his students at Loyola University Medical School in Chicago, Jake had absorbed everything he had to offer and wanted more. He had become not only her mentor, but a friend and confidant as well. As colleagues through the years, each valued the expertise and perspective of the other, and they often called upon each other for consultation. *Maybe, just maybe, Philip can see something we've missed,* Jake thought as the elevator glided down to the mezzanine level.

As usual, Philip's presentation was brilliant, cutting edge, and enthusiastically received. He eagerly fielded the barrage of questions from excited colleagues. Jake stood across the room smiling, knowing he would devote the full measure of his time and expertise to every question. Catching his attention, she pointed to the lounge door, then to herself and mouthed "later." Then she made her way through the crowd to wait for him in the bar until he was free for dinner.

It will be so good to visit with Philip. He always could calm the storms in my mind. Maybe a fresh pair of eyes, especially with Philip's acuity, will see what I'm missing. I'm too close to it. And too distracted. I'm glad Kalani and Philip wrangled me into taking these few days off.

As if on cue, her thoughts wandered to Cara. *Should I call her? Maybe invite her to lunch tomorrow? Admit it, Jake, you want to see her.* An uncomfortable feeling of having to justify herself ran through Jake's mind. *Well, I should at least check to see how that wound on her side is, and if she had the stitches removed.*

She was on her second margarita and beginning to feel more relaxed than she had in a long time when she heard a feminine voice with a soft Irish lilt talking to the hostess. "I'll be in the lounge, Rebecca. I'm expecting company about eight. Could you please show my guest to my table? Oh! Before I forget, how did your son's birthday party go last night? Did he like the new PlayStation?"

"I'll say he did, Ms. Quinn! And the game you gave him to go with it was a big hit. Thank you so much." Rebecca smiled with a feigned look of exasperation. "He was the undefeated champion until way past his bedtime and was up this morning before dawn, at it again. Sorry you couldn't make it. Maybe one night soon you'll come for dinner?"

"Oh my, I would have loved to come, your son sounds wonderful. And one night soon, I promise, I'll come for a bit of dinner. Just as soon as I get settled in with the new job."

"Well, Danny and I are looking forward to it," Rebecca smiled, jotting down the instructions. "Will it be just the one guest, Ms. Quinn?"

"Yes, but we agreed, please call me McKenzie." She offered a smile as bright as her emerald green eyes. "This is a very special dinner tonight; could we have a table with the view of the mountains and a bottle of your best wine?"

"I'll see to it myself Ms. Qui—McKenzie. Do you have a particular wine in mind?"

"Hmm, I trust your judgment, and Rebecca, will you send a few bottles of the Guinness to my suite?"

"Consider it done." Before turning her attention to a couple waiting to be seated for dinner, Rebecca smiled and whispered to McKenzie, "Good luck, I hope you have a very special evening."

An impish grin pulled at McKenzie's hopeful eyes. "If you're lucky enough to be Irish, then you're lucky enough. But thank you, Rebecca, I'll accept your blessing."

Glancing into the mirror behind the bar, Jake watched as the attractive strawberry blonde sat next to her. She noted the expensive, tailored silk suit that complimented the petite woman's figure. Her eyes strayed to the intricate silver necklace the woman wore. She knew the symbol, an ancient Celtic cross, and she had seen something like it before...somewhere.

"Evening, Ms. Quinn, what can I get you tonight?" the bartender asked.

"A vodka tonic," turning toward Jake with a friendly smile and a glance at her drink, "and another margarita for my friend here." She offered her hand to Jake. "Hi, I'm McKenzie."

Jake couldn't help but smile at the open friendliness of the attractive woman. Accepting the gesture, she introduced herself. "Jacquelyn, thank you. That's an interesting hint of an accent you have. Northern Ireland, Belfast?"

"You have a good ear to be that specific. It's been a long time now, and I was educated here in the States. Have you spent time in Ireland?"

Not really wanting to explain how or why she could pinpoint an accent or a dialect with such accuracy, Jake hedged. Besides, tonight she was not the FBI's Dr. Jacquelyn Biscayne. She was just a woman sharing a drink.

"I was fortunate to have spent some time there."

"Are you staying here at the Radisson, too?" McKenzie asked after tasting her drink.

Stirring her margarita, Jake answered, "Yes, just for the weekend, though; I'm afraid it's back to work on Monday. You?"

"For a while, until I find some serious time to look for an apartment or house. I just relocated from Boston. Learning a new city and job has kept me quite busy, but it's comfortable here at the Radisson. They've made it an easy transition and a real welcome to Tucson."

"Do you know anyone here, any friends who can show you places to look and places not to look?" Jake inquired.

Cocking her head and with an arch of one eyebrow, McKenzie allowed her eyes to travel over the woman sitting next to her. *What a striking woman! If I weren't so smitten with Cara, she definitely would warrant my interest.*

"I do have a good friend here, and I have a reputable realtor searching for me. But I've been draggin' my feet. I am hoping to renew a friendship and possibly..." A pensive look crept across McKenzie's face. Her voice drifted off. After a brief silence, the warm smile returned. "Now tell me a bit about your wonderful Arizona."

Jake and McKenzie rattled on as if they were old friends until Rebecca reappeared in the lounge.

"Your guest is here. I've put in your request for the special wine, and the Guinness is already in your suite." Rebecca started to leave but turned back. "Oh, and you have the best table in the house, beautiful views of Mt. Lemmon and the sunset tonight."

"Thank you, Rebecca," McKenzie said, blushing slightly. Turning her attention back to Jake, she asked, "What are you doing for lunch tomorrow, Jacquelyn? Please have lunch with me." She laughed. "Besides, I need you to continue painting all the magnificent colors of this splendid state for me."

Jake thought for a second. *Hmm...Philip's presentation isn't until three o'clock tomorrow.* "Yes, I would like that. Could we make it, say, about eleven thirty?"

"Perfect, where shall we meet?" McKenzie asked.

"Here in the lobby. Now an important decision," Jake said quite seriously. "Do you want to go to this marvelous little pub that serves melt-in-your-mouth boxties and warm stout or try some authentic Mexican food?"

McKenzie's eyes danced with mischief. "Well, as they say, when in Rome!"

Laughing along with McKenzie, Jake couldn't help but feel a genuine liking for the impish Irish beauty.

Jake and Philip were enjoying an after-dinner coffee when she spotted McKenzie across the restaurant heading from the direction of the ladies' room. She couldn't suppress her curiosity as her eyes followed the woman back to her table. *Hmm, I wonder what her date looks like? She seemed to be on cloud nine...with a mission.* As McKenzie sat down, Jake realized the decorative plants completely obscured her view of the dinner guest. When she saw McKenzie slip off her shoe and thrust her foot toward the leg, she presumed, of whoever was sitting across from her, Jake chuckled to herself. *Yes, my Irish friend is on a mission tonight!* Quickly, she returned her attention back to Philip.

"I appreciate you agreeing to look over the evidence I gave you, Philip. I just can't shake the feeling that I'm missing something."

"Could be you're not missing anything, Jake. Have you thought of that? You expect so much of yourself. You have some good DNA with this last murder, and if this guy is caught you'll nail him."

"Key word, *if* we catch him. How many has he killed, how many more? It just isn't these three we happened upon. There are more, Philip, and he's been at it a long time. I just feel it."

Cara was unsuccessfully trying to hide her amusement at McKenzie's flirting as she reached down and caught a foot. "Behave yourself, Kenzie. If you haven't noticed, we're all grown up and not in your father's pub here!"

With a fetching smile, McKenzie leaned across the table, her green eyes sparkling. "I seem to recall that you never used to mind where we were. Ya haven't gone and gotten all serious on me now, have ya? And might I add, I haven't seen you smile all week." McKenzie softened her voice. "That is what little I have seen of you. I didn't think you were going to accept my invitation to dinner, ya know the one I've extended every day this week. If I were pressed to come up with a reason, I would think you've been avoiding me."

She held her breath, needing to know. "Is there a reason, Cara, for you to avoid me? Are you with someone, seeing someone?"

Cara searched the lovely face of her friend and former lover, remembering the endearing qualities of McKenzie Quinn. The outgoing, outspoken barmaid who became her mentor. The confident law student who without pretense or airs bowled them over at Harvard by graduating number one in her class. She remembered the hours they spent studying and working at the Keltic Knot and the night they became lovers and the tearful day after graduation when she flew home to California, both women pledging to keep in touch. There wasn't a reason in the world to avoid McKenzie; they had been good together, no promises were made, and each had seen others during the last year of college.

Now, looking at the desire written on McKenzie's face, Cara realized she had isolated herself too long, living with the guilt of Stephen's death. A reason to avoid McKenzie? No reason at all, except maybe wanting something unobtainable in the face of a hazel-eyed untouchable.

Cara reached over and held her friend's hand. "No, my friend. I'm not with or seeing anyone, and I am truly glad to see you."

Chapter Eight

"The money! Did you collect all the money?"

"*Sí*, all but three, *jefe*." The man's voice and jaw quivered, causing a drop of sweat to trickle from his upper lip down the corner of his mouth. Fear pressed at his darting eyes and immobilized him. He heard a quiet but strange laugh as the other glowered heartlessly at him down the length of his aquiline nose. Lowering his eyes, he failed to see the hard leather handle of the whip slice toward him even though he heard it a split second before it struck him. The blow crashed into his cheek, splitting flesh and shattering bone.

Instinctively, he knew to make no sound, no movement, or he would suffer more—how could he doubt the stories he had heard, standing here now in the presence of such evil? For not collecting all the money from the illegals, one *guía* had a dagger run through the palm of his hand. And when he screamed out his pain, his tongue was cut out. Another had been gutted like a pig, as the story went, when he was rolled in a cantina and the money he'd collected from a shipment of illegals was stolen. Without a movement the man stood, head hung in silence, waiting as blood streaked down his face.

The merciless hand of terror suddenly gripped the air in the warehouse. "Who did not pay?" queried the deceptively calm voice from the shadows as if he had just asked the time of day.

Still with his eyes to the ground, the trembling man choked out, "The old man, his daughter, and two *peónes* from the village of El Picacho."

As the shadow voice materialized from a dim corner of the warehouse, boding evil permeated the atmosphere, stifling all thought, all hope of survival. The *diablo* moved to the grimy window where he stood transfixed, staring out, his face void of any semblance of emotion. Except the eyes. If the eyes truly are the mirror into one's soul, here stood the embodiment of the foulest evil. Repeatedly, the slap of the whip handle against a palm of the man called *La Serpiente* cut into the stillness of the hot warehouse.

Waiting with his eyes still lowered, the smuggler felt his heart pounding at his chest, the coppery taste of blood streaming into his mouth from his injured cheek. He was not a coward. Running illegals and drugs over the border as his father had before him, he knew the dangers, the risks. Yet he stood now paralyzed with fear. He knew the stories of *La Serpiente*, the serpent—all trembled before him as the blood stilled in their veins. Now he had seen the man behind the stories. He was close enough to smell his aftershave mixed with the faint hint of tequila. Close enough to hear the squeak of leather as *La Serpiente* ground his boot heel into the dirt floor of the warehouse. Squeezing his eyes shut, the *coyote* silently mouthed a plea to the Holy Mother, unaware of the flies hungrily swarming his bloody face.

The voice, now tinged with annoyance, sent shivers down his spine. "Separate them, put the girl in my van. Tell the old man he will go another time when the daughter can pay his fare. Use one other to load the cargo. Then get rid of him, *comprende*?

Without raising his eyes, the man nodded his understanding and whispered, "*Sí, jefe*." He could feel the evil burning his skin. A sudden rush of wind, a cracking sound, and the sensation of warm liquid running from his ear brought the man's hand to his head. In horror, he felt for his ear, then realized the top half was gone. Confused, his mind running franticly, he moaned in pain.

Laughter as sinister as the fires of hell pummeled his consciousness. If he could hang on just a little longer... "Flies," he heard through the rush of blood through his neck and pain on the side of his face, then another crack of the whip that had become *La Serpiente's* trademark. It burned his cheek as it sliced through the flesh, dissecting a fly in the process. Grimacing, he waited for what seemed like an eternity in the mouldy air of the warehouse, tasting his own blood. The shriek of a hawk pierced the silence, but he heard no movement or sound near him.

Gradually, he opened his eyes. *La Serpiente* had vanished. The drug-running *coyote* quivered as he lost control of his bladder. He sank to his knees, his legs no longer able to hold him upright. Sucking in a ragged breath, he crossed himself and gave thanks he was still alive.

The old man was hesitant about being separated from his daughter. He wanted her to stay with him until they could scrape together the rest of the price. With determination and pride, Lupe reached through the darkness to find her father's hand.

"Papa, I am strong, I can work. I have promise of a job in Phoenix at the packing plant where Ernesto works. I can send for you in a short time, we will work and wait for the next amnesty offer. It will be good. We can start a new life, Papa. Have a little place, just the two of us. You can have your garden, and we will save to open our own place where you can make the tamales, the carne asada we all love." She hugged the frail old man. "Papa, you make the best salsa I have ever tasted. We will have a life. I promise it will not be long. Go stay with Enrique. I know you will be safe there."

The girl's voice cracked with sadness, and her belly growled with hunger. She had so many hopes and dreams.

Yet, the old man had no one else to ask for money. He had saved for years, working seven days a week at any job he could find, to get enough *dinero* to pay the price of the *coyote*. Many times when he had reached the price, it was only to hear, "Not enough, old man!" But this time he finally had enough for the *coyote*. He had handed all his savings over, and now he was told it wasn't enough, that it was only enough for one.

In the vile darkness, the stench of vomit, stale urine, and body odor made him cringe. He clutched his child to his heart while tears streamed from his eyes as much from the repulsive smells as from his fear and sense of utter helplessness. If he refused his daughter this opportunity for a new life in the United States, would there be another chance? Or would he condemn her to a life of poverty and hopelessness in Mexico? All in life that mattered or had any importance to the old man was this girl, his child, his beautiful Lupe holding his hand in the dark.

The door of the "guest house" shed opened, letting in a coolness in spite of the over one-hundred-degree temperature outside. The *pollos* were kept locked in the darkness, cramped in like cattle going to slaughter. There was not enough room for everyone to sit or lay down, so they took turns standing then sitting. For three days, only tortillas and water were thrown in to them. Many passed out from dehydration and the unbearable heat in the overcrowded shed. The group of illegal border crossers stood shielding their eyes from the bright sun, uneasy about what was happening and unsure of what was to come.

The smuggler with a bloody bandage on his ear motioned the *polleros* to begin loading the two vans, one with the illegals that had paid, the other with the tied bundles from the corner of the warehouse. A man who had been unable to pay any more was shoved along brutally toward the old man.

He cowered against the hot metal of the truck, his body fear-wracked. But the dismay of going back without his money to his wife and children, who had very little, gave him the courage to speak.

"Please, *señor*, my money, it is all I have. My family...if I can not go to *el otro lado*, across to the other side to work, they will be hungry."

The *coyote* smiled through rotted, tobacco-stained teeth, and the frightened man smiled back, some of his fear relieved.

"*Sí, mi amigo*, so it is a refund you wish?" he asked, as he pulled his pistol from his belt and shot the man once between the eyes. Callously, he called one of his men over. "Throw him with the other one."

Then he lowered his voice and whispered something to the man before turning to the terrified illegals. He narrowed his eyes in warning, the message as chilling as the voice. "The desert, she holds many secrets."

Icy tendrils of terror stilled the land and wove inside the hearts of the defenseless immigrants, all of them feeling the cold fingers of death, wondering if it would be their day, too, to die.

The glare of eerie yellow-green monitor lights illuminated Matt's haggard face as he sat anxiously in the command center van. For days, the Border Patrol had surreptitiously planned Operation Jack Rabbit, hoping that they would land a serious blow to a major Mexican drug-trafficking cartel that had plagued the Nogales, Arizona/Nogales, Sonora border sector for months. The Border Patrol was stretched to the limits trying to monitor the vast area, especially with the increase in border security and inland checkpoints since 9/11. Many trucks, legitimate and not, had been put out of commission since the beef-up, and they had made considerable dents in the drug trade on the Santa Cruz County border. But drugs still poured over, like ants swarming a picnic, smuggled into the U.S. hidden in everything from tomatoes to microchips.

Still, the loss of profits had many a trafficker nervous, and when they lost millions of dollars in a single night, the retaliation was predictable and ruthless. When a runner lost a cartel's money, he faced harsh reprisals, if not death. Escape was no option. Even if he managed to save his own life, his family was terrorized or held captive until he returned and faced the organization and his own fate at the hands of the cartel *jefe*.

Border Patrol Agents lay in wait to snare the front men of one of the most merciless organizations, along with a purportedly massive payload of cocaine and heroin. A deep-cover federal agent had tipped the Border Patrol to the huge shipments coming across that week, and if the information was even half right, the smugglers' plan was to simultaneously assault the border at no fewer than five different points between Nogales and Naco.

But Matt was confident in his agents. During their training, recruits were taught this type of mission, and the task force had run simulations all week in preparation. Still, he felt the prickle at the hairs on the back of his neck, an errant thought jabbing at the back of his mind: *Catch this drug smuggler, and we catch our killer.*

Matt reached for the radio. "Checkpoint two, ya there?"

Alejandro pressed the button on his radio. "Check."

"Just got movement at one o'clock. You see anything?"

Stationed high on a rocky escarpment, Alejandro scanned the desert below him through the night vision glasses. He picked up the motion as plainly as if it were high noon. "Got it, *coyotes*, four-legged kind. And heads popping up down your way to sector five."

"Keep alert, if it's gonna happen tonight, should be soon, before daylight."

With the disembodied voice of his commander echoing in his ears, Alejandro settled back behind the cover of a hackberry bush and motioned an "okay" sign to another agent down a ways.

Matt knew the dangers of spreading his men out this thinly, two to a checkpoint, but it was the best he could do. Besides, the sensors placed along the crossing areas would give them an advantage. He reflected on his decision to have the scheduled night border air surveillance called down to standby, just to be on the safe side. It shouldn't spook the traffickers off or draw extra attention since air surveillance never followed a set schedule, needing to be inconspicuous by their very presence. Fully comprehending the dangers of the entire mission and his men's safety, Matt was also concerned about the illegals. If the smugglers sensed they were in danger of losing their load of drugs, they would create a diversion, using them like sacrificial lambs to the slaughter.

"Too many lives at stake tonight," he mumbled and crossed himself.

Hours ticked by with only the regular radio checks from the patrol sectors breaking the monotony of watching the monitors. Matt felt his eyes drooping. Surveying the screens first, he then poured a cup of cold, black coffee and stood up outside the van to stretch his back. Suddenly the still desert burst to life with the shrilling screech of the monitors, followed by a chorus of not too distant gunshots. Matt dropped his cup and dove back into the van, simultaneously snatching the radio handset and scanning the monitors. Sector five was swarming with activity, and there were shots everywhere now.

"Hector, Roberto! God damn it, what's going on out there? Sector five, come in! Air patrol, you copy?"

"Roger that, Night Hawke. Two units on standby, over."

"I need lights and agents in sector five. Shots fired, extensive sensor activity. Two agents not responding. What's your ETA? Over."

"Five minutes. Over."

"I'm going in. Let me know when you locate my men, Night Hawke. Out."

"Will do."

Grabbing his rifle and checking his 9-mm and extra clips, Matt ran to his Jeep. Keying his radio, he ordered, "All agents sound off and proceed to sector five! Repeat, all agents advance to five!" Throwing the radio on the seat, Matt tore across the night desert.

When he arrived on the scene, it was chaos. Federal agents were rounding up illegals and tending to the wounded or covering the dead. Night Hawke leader, Agent Malloy, approached Matt.

"One of the survivors said they were told to run for freedom, for safety. These guys knew the sensors were there because they herded the illegals across directly in the path of the arrays. Then they shot them in the back just as they tripped the alarms. The bastards used them as bait to draw us off, Matt."

A sickening taste rose into his throat. "Where are Hector and Roberto?"

Malloy drew a deep, ragged breath. "Their throats were garroted. Looks like they were taken by surprise before the smugglers set the illegals loose as decoys to draw us to this area. Funny, it's like they knew exactly where we were and how we would play this, Matt. It must have been one hell of an important shipment."

Matt's emotions flashed across his face, threatening to overtake his sensibilities, but he knew he had to check his rising anger and get the mess under control. "Is everyone accounted for?"

"From what I can tell, you have two more missing from sector two, Alejandro and Josh. And Matt, the undercover agent down in Naco—well, he's dead, too. Mexican police found him late tonight lying in a ditch, murdered. His head had been smashed in with rocks."

Matt felt like he'd been kicked in the stomach. "Rottenfuckingbastards. They will die slow." He turned and headed to his Jeep to get the radio. "Alejandro, do you copy? Josh! Come in if you copy."

Leaning against the Jeep for support, Matt was afraid they would never answer.

Malloy stood beside him quietly for a minute, then asked, "Is there anything you need, Matt?"

Matt looked out across the desert at the dawning of another day with hatred burning in his gut. "Do you believe in the darkness in men's souls, Malloy?"

"What?"

"Nothing, just thinking out loud." Matt shifted his eyes around to meet Malloy's. "And yes, I need Jake here ASAP. She's up in Tucson; Kalani knows how to contact her. Secure the area and get her people out here. I want roadblocks on every road and pig trail leading out of this goddamn state. Get more air support down here. Make the calls to the FBI, Malloy. I'm going to sector two."

Matt headed toward his Jeep, then stopped and turned back to Malloy.

"Something else, Matt?"

"Put in a call to the Shadow Wolves at Tohono O'odham Indian Reservation. Tell 'em I need a couple trackers out here." Matt's voice broke for the first time. "Tell 'em we lost..." *How many? two or...*"Tell 'em two of our own, confirmed, two unaccounted for." Matt steadied his voice.

"You better tell Craig one of the missing is Alejandro. He'll want to know if he has to tell the family."

"Oh Jesus! That's right, they're brothers. Damn. Go do what you need to do, Matt. I'll take care of the calls."

Matt slammed to a stop at the marker for sector two and walked cautiously toward the outcropping of mesquite and hackberry where his men were last positioned. A sickening realization tore at his gut with each step. As he got closer, he heard a weak disembodied voice from behind the rocks. "Help me."

Forgetting the danger, Matt crawled over the rocks to the voice and saw from the green uniform and Border Patrol insignias that it was one of his agents down on the ground. He was hurt badly, and there was a pool of blood underneath him.

Matt keyed his lapel mike while checking the agent's condition. "Malloy! Get a paramedic over here, now! It's Alejandro and he's hurt bad!" Cradling Alejandro's head in his arms, Matt tried to keep his voice calm and free of the panic he felt rising. "Damn, you're a mess, kid."

"Hey boss," Alejandro whispered and coughed. Frothy blood oozed down his chin.

"Don't talk, *amigo*," Matt said as he pressed his hands over the gunshot wounds in Alejandro's chest and shoulder.

"Matt...don't squeeze...my shoulder..." Alejandro gasped out in a wheezy whisper. "It's fuckin' killing me..." He had a slight smile on his face while the tears trickled down his temples. "Matt..."

"Save your strength. You can talk later."

"No...gotta tell you..."

Before he could finish, Alejandro sucked in a rattling breath. He never let it out.

"Goddamn it, boy, don't you die on me! Malloy, where are the fucking paramedics!"

Frantically, Matt started CPR. He never heard Malloy or the paramedic calling his name. It was only when the Night Hawke leader caught his shoulder and shook him that Matt realized they were there.

"He's gone, Matt. You can stop now."

"No. He's gonna make it! Alejandro's not a quitter."

"We all know that, Matt, but for Christ's sake, leave him be."

Matt jerked away from Malloy's grasp and stalked over to his Jeep. Pounding his fist into the hood, he yelled, "So help me God, whoever did this, when I catch him, I'm gonna kill the son of a bitch with my bare hands!"

Jake sat staring into her coffee in deep thought. "Can you come to visit for a few days, Philip, or do you need to get back right away?"

Philip knew her well enough to sense she had something on her mind besides the case. "I would like to, Jake, but I have a commitment in L.A. that will take some time. LAPD has been revamping their forensic procedures and policies, and they've asked me to head up the process. I've agreed, on a temporary basis, that is."

Philip paused, taking a long look at his friend before he reached to cover her hand with his. "How are you really, Jake? It's been over two years now. Are the dreams any better?"

Jake placed her other hand on top of Philip's, and with a warm smile and soft voice, she reassured him. "You're such a good friend, Philip. I don't know if I would have made it after Sam and Dad's deaths if it hadn't been for you. Have I ever thanked you for being there, for being such a dear friend?"

"Oh I think so, a few times as I recall," he chuckled as he put his arm around her shoulders and pulled her in for a hug.

Jake was vaguely aware of the staccato click of approaching footsteps and was pleasantly surprised when she heard McKenzie's accent.

"Jacquelyn." McKenzie smiled down at Jake and Philip. "I see you're enjoying the evening as well."

Jake turned in her chair to greet McKenzie. And—and Cara?

McKenzie put her arm around Cara's slender waist, smiling lovingly up at her. "Jacquelyn, I want you to meet my friend, Cara."

The moment Jake had turned to greet them, Cara's heart raced. Now, as she looked at Philip's arm around Jake and Jake holding his hand, it was pounding out of her chest. Her legs went weak, and the color drained from her face. All she could see were those hazel eyes staring back at her, the eyes that had haunted her dreams as well as her wakening hours. There was no doubt now. The reason for the restless emptiness she'd had since returning to Tucson was Jake. She missed her, and for the first time she honestly had to admit to herself that her feelings had evolved beyond friendship. Right now, the loud roar of jealousy was tearing her up. But it couldn't drown the sound of her breaking heart.

Cara—Cara and McKenzie? Jake couldn't pull her bewildered eyes away from the piercing brown ones she had longed to see. Her mind was numb. A peculiar sensation washed over her that she didn't know what to make of. Her irrepressibly rapid heartbeat, her difficulty catching her breath.

No, this is all wrong. Why do I feel this way? It's none of my business who she is—is friends with. Why do I feel so— so...damn. Oh God, could this be jealousy? I think I care for her more than just as a friend. Breathe, Jake, just breathe.

With bottom lip quivering, Jake forced a smile and leaned in closer to Philip, not wanting Cara or McKenzie to know how upset she was. She squeezed his hand tightly, silently praying he would go along. "Oh, I already know the notorious Cara Vittore. How are the stitches?"

An unnerving quiet settled in for a moment while Cara's brown eyes searched hazel ones.

"The good doctor here wields a wicked needle—but she sits a good horse. Nice to see you...too, Jake."

Philip stood and offered his hand to McKenzie. "I'm Philip Raynard, Ms...?"

"McKenzie Quinn, pleased to meet you, Philip. Are you staying here at the Radisson?"

"Yes, I am for a few days. Tucson has always been one of my favorite places." He glanced over at Jake. "Even more so now."

McKenzie noticed Cara had not taken her eyes off Jake during the entire exchange. "Well, we'll be on our way. Don't forget our lunch date tomorrow, Jacquelyn."

Jake tore her eyes from Cara. "Uh...no, no I won't. Have a good evening."

Philip considered the heavy breath Jake exhaled as the two women left the dining room. "Anything you want to talk about?"

Jake's brow was drawn into a tight knot. She thought, *All I want right now is to get the hell out of here before I make a fool of myself and start crying,* but she shook her head no.

"Would you mind if we call it a night, Philip?"

He studied his friend's face before answering. "Meet me for breakfast, kiddo. Now go get a good night's sleep, we'll talk tomorrow."

Alone in the darkness of her room with only the light of a full moon streaming through the window, Jake couldn't get the image of Cara and McKenzie out of her mind—or to be more accurate, Cara with McKenzie.

They could be just friends. No, just wishful thinking, Jake. The look in McKenzie's eye was not just friendship, and the arm around Cara's waist was all too familiar being there. Hard as she tried, the picture of Cara caressing McKenzie, kissing and making love to her, disturbed her considerably more than her rational mind told her it should. Frustrated, Jake sprang off the couch, pacing the floor in a one-woman tirade.

"Damn, woman, it was better when I hated you! Besides, you're a woman! What's that all about, Jake? You've been lusting over a *woman,* and obviously it has not been mutual. And the strangest thing is I like McKenzie; she's attractive, so I can understand why—or if—Cara would...take her as a—a...lover. Oh! Damn, I promised to meet her for lunch."

Groaning, she snatched her shoes off and hurled them across the room, knocking the receiver off the phone in the process. She stripped off her clothes, poured herself a glass of wine, and headed to the sunken Jacuzzi to soak. Turning on the jets, she eased herself down into the swirling, warm water with the image of Cara and McKenzie spinning in her mind.

Cara looked out over the lights of Tucson from McKenzie's suite. She kept replaying the scene in the restaurant over in her mind.

Why did I think there was something between us? She's straight. I knew it, but I fell anyway. I wanted to go to her that night at the ranch. I wanted to touch her, to hold her. Be honest with yourself, Cara, you wanted to make love with her. And you still do. There was something in her eyes...I know it. I could feel it. She looked pretty chummy with that guy tonight, though. Damn, I wish I had never met her!

McKenzie walked over with two bottles of Guinness, handing one to Cara.

"Thanks." Cara smiled, holding it up. "You remembered, my favorite."

McKenzie took a sip of her beer, running her finger along Cara's arm, never taking her eyes off Cara's. "I remember a lot of things."

"You do, huh?"

"Oh yeah, I do."

"It's been a long time, Kenzie."

McKenzie's arms stole around Cara's waist. "Exactly. Any reason it has to be any longer?"

Cara could feel the warmth of McKenzie's small body pressing against hers. Remembering the comfort and familiarity, the unquestionable way she always responded to her touch, she was aware of the heat spreading through her chest and downward as McKenzie kissed the soft hollow of her throat. It had been too long since a woman had touched her this way, too long since she had simply felt. All the anger and frustration, all the need and desire that had been awakened for Jake would not be denied tonight, and McKenzie was offering to satisfy that need.

Just after midnight, Cara lay listening to the rhythmic raindrops spattering against the windows, her thoughts not on the beautiful, desirable woman lying next to her with whom she had just made love. Instead, all she could see was a certain unquestionably irritating yet enticing blonde doctor. She gently untangled herself from McKenzie's embrace and slipped out of bed. The room was unfamiliar in the midnight shadows as she stood naked by the window gathering her thoughts, allowing the sound of the rain to soothe her. In the surreal light of night, it seemed unimaginable that she had used her friend as she had, knowing McKenzie wanted more than one night for old time's sake. Lightning crackled just as she looked back at the naked figure in the bed. Cara sighed and turned again to the city lights glistening in the rain. Could she break her friend's heart? Could she say, *well it's been nice, let's do it again sometime?*

"Tell me why you're here?" McKenzie's voice broke the silence.

"What kind of question is that?"

"Well, it's just that you're here, but you're not here," came the softly accented voice.

Cara looked at her for some moments before she spoke in a voice that was even, but strained. "God, Kenzie, I'm so sorry. It's just...I don't know."

"What's Jacquelyn to you, Cara?"

Cara visibly stiffened at the mention of Jake's name. She turned to stare out at the rain. "What makes you think she's anything to me?"

"Oh, maybe the way you looked at her earlier this evening. Or the fact that you called out her name tonight."

Cara covered her face with her hands and moaned, "I'm so sorry, so sorry."

McKenzie studied her friend, the woman she had never stopped loving, knowing Cara's anguish was real. Pushing her own hurt down, she patted the bed next to her. "C'mere, love, and tell me what this is all about."

Cara lay in her friend's arms and tried to explain about Jake. About the murders and her involvement. How they started out sparring like two boxers and the near-death experience in the desert and how Jake took her home and patched her up.

"Have you told her how you feel?" McKenzie asked quietly.

"No, I wasn't sure how I felt, I guess. Until I saw her tonight with the boyfriend."

McKenzie hesitated, knowing what she was about to tell Cara could possibly end any hope of them being together. "That wasn't her boyfriend, love. He's a colleague and an old friend of hers here doing a lecture series, and Jacquelyn asked him to consult on a case she has been working on."

Cara sat quickly up in bed. "How do you know all this, Kenzie?"

"I told you we met in the lounge tonight and we, well, hit it off, we shared a bit." McKenzie looked selflessly at Cara. "It's possible she might be feeling the same thing you are. And jumping to the same conclusions you did, I might add."

A puzzled look crossed Cara's face. "What do you mean?" Then as she glanced at their naked bodies, the realization came clear. "Oh Lord, and it's justified!"

Cara hopped out of bed and gathered her clothes. "Do you know what room she's in?"

Holding in her tears, McKenzie answered, "214, love."

Cara approached the bed and took her friend's hand as she kissed her cheek. "Thank you, my friend. Can you ever forgive me?"

McKenzie loved the woman standing there in the dim light before her. And she had since that first day in the Keltic Knot when Cara cradled her guitar and sang her mother's favorite Irish song. *I should have gone after her; I should have found her sooner.*

McKenzie reached up to caress Cara's face with both hands before she softly kissed her lips. "Hey, if you need anything I'll be here. Now go."

Jake had fallen asleep to the lull of the Jacuzzi, but the insistent pounding at the door jolted her awake. Hurrying out of the water, she wrapped the terry robe the hotel provided around her wet body and made her way through the dark suite. *Now who could that be this time of night?* Cautiously, she looked through the peephole to see Cara running a hand through her hair. Surprised, Jake leaned against the door, not wanting to open it. Again, Cara knocked, and Jake slowly unlocked and opened the door. The two women stood in the hallway staring at each other in absolute silence until Cara finally spoke.

"Jake, I know it's late, but please, I need to talk to you."

Jake took in Cara's disheveled appearance, including the bruise on her neck. The old animosity as well as a new jealousy twisted inside her. Staring directly at Cara's neck, she lashed out. "Tough night, Counselor?"

"It's not what you think...exactly. Please, Jake, can I come in? I want to explain about tonight."

"You don't owe me any explanation. What you do and with whom is no concern of mine. I don't think we have anything further to say to each other so if you'll excuse me, it's late."

Jake shifted to close the door, but Cara braced her foot against it. She reached out and held Jake around her waist. The move caught Jake off guard, and she instinctively raised her forearms against Cara's chest in protest just as Cara's lips found hers in a slow, tender kiss. Breathless, Jake felt the softness of the lips on hers.

"What are you doing?" she moaned.

"I'm kissing you."

She could feel Cara's tongue gently brushing her lips, and she opened further to meet a passionate tongue exploring hers. The two stood in the embrace with an awareness only of each other until the sound of someone clearing his throat startled them apart.

"Sorry, ladies, but I have an urgent message for a Dr. Biscayne. Is one of you...?"

Pushing away from Cara, Jake reached for the folded paper. "I'm Dr. Biscayne."

Jake paled as she read the note. Angrily, she turned to the messenger. "Why wasn't this call put through to me?"

"Sorry, Doctor, your room phone has been busy, and the woman who left this message said it was urgent and to tell you to turn your cell on."

She remembered turning off her cell phone during dinner. With all her emotions running high, she had apparently forgotten to turn it back on after returning to her room. Jake spun around and hurried into the room. "I need to go."

Cara was right on her heels. "What is it, Jake? What's happened?"

"Matt needs me. A drug stakeout went bad tonight. Two of Matt's men confirmed killed and two unaccounted for." Her voice cracked and caught in her throat. "One is Alejandro."

Sucking in a lungful of air, Cara squeezed her eyes shut a moment, then walked over to the stunned doctor. "How are you getting there?"

Jake didn't answer right away. For just a split second, her mind was reliving another time of loss. That unforgettable day in front of her apartment when minutes felt like they were stretched into hours, the day Sam died, the day her world exploded and her nightmares began.

Sensing Jake's pain, Cara gently touched her arm. "Are you driving back to Nogales?"

"BP is sending a chopper, it should be here by the time I get to the helipad on the roof."

"Go get dressed, I'll pack your things." Cara shoved Jake toward the bathroom and started tossing clothes into the suitcase.

Just as Jake came out of the bathroom tucking a white shirt into crisp Levi's, Cara snapped her cell phone shut. Impatiently, Jake pulled her boots on. A profound weariness etched her face. "Cara I...we..."

"This is not the time or place, Jake. We need to go, the helicopter is on the roof."

Jake looked questioningly at her. "We?"

"I'm going with you."

Jake's long, determined stride took her to the door in seconds. "No, you're not going with me, and you're right, we don't have the time for this."

And with that, she was out the door, hurrying to the elevator that would take her to the helipad. Once on the roof, she braced herself against the sheets of rain thrown around the roof from the chopper blades. Agent Malloy held the door of the helicopter open against the blowing wind.

"Where's the other passenger?" he yelled above the thud of whirling blades.

Jake lobbed her bag into the chopper and climbed in. "I'm it, let's go."

Malloy continued to yell above the relentless noise of wind, blade, and rain. "I have orders from the attorney general to pick up a Cara Vittore, too, Jake. We received a directive giving her any and all access in this investigation."

"God damn it, Malloy, get this thing in the air now!" Jake demanded.

"No can do, Jake. I got my orders to wait for Vittore."

As if on cue, the chopper door opened and the tall lawyer climbed in, dressed in a black pin-striped Italian suit that was soaking wet from the pelting rain. Void of emotion, brown smoldering eyes met Malloy's. "I'm Cara Vittore."

Jake wanted to lash out at her, to scream at her, to blame her for the ache in her heart. She wanted to order her to go back where she belonged...to stay in her safe life and leave her the hell alone. She wanted this woman out of her thoughts, but most of all she did not want to care. She couldn't even look at the woman sitting beside her as the chopper lifted off from the roof. Instead, a cold shiver coursed down her spine and settled in the pit of her stomach. It was the same feeling she had had two years ago sitting on the witness stand—when she first laid eyes on Cara Vittore.

Chapter Nine

The moonlit figure crouched low, distributing his body weight equally on the backs of his legs, his arms resting across both knees. Alejandro's lifeblood, the same blood that ran through his own veins, stained the earth crimson at his boots. Patiently, he waited for the first streaks of dawn before setting out to track the cold-blooded killer who had stolen the soul of his young brother.

Kalani stood silently behind him. The sorrow and angst in her heart was evident in her voice, which was nothing more than a shaky whisper. "It will be daylight soon, Craig. I'm sorry we had to wait. We'll start gathering evidence just as soon as it is light enough, then we'll take him home, my friend."

The tracker nodded slightly, his dark eyes never wavering from the east and the soon-to-be-rising sun. He was a warrior possessing the skills that had been taught and handed down by the old ones of a lost culture to track his quarry the old-fashioned way, by following silent, invisible clues. He was Native American and a Shadow Wolf, one of the elite U.S Customs tracking units whose first job was to patrol the three-million-acre Tohono O'odham Reservation. But the Shadow Wolves were also part of the front line of defense along the seventy-six miles of border. For thirty years, Shadow Wolves had tracked the Mexican smugglers and confiscated no small percentage of their never-ending flow of contraband, people, and drugs that had been crossing into the United States since the international border was created by the Gadsden Treaty in 1853.

It had just gotten personal. The cold, lifeless body of the young Border Patrol agent lay where he had fallen, alone in his own blood on the desert floor. For the first time since he was a boy, the man cried silent tears.

"Rest now, brother, for your death will be avenged."

Rising to his feet, he touched the small grey feather pinned to his shirt, focused his eyes on the quickening eastern sky, and let his voice pierce the deceptive serenity of the quiet desert night. "In brightest day, in darkest night, no evil shall escape my sight, for I am the Shadow Wolf."

"We're about ten minutes out, Jake. Where do you want us to set down?" Malloy's voice edged its way into Jake's thoughts, distracting her from the anger boiling within. She wasn't ready to let go of it, but knew she had to. It was an intrusion that she could not afford if she were to concentrate all her efforts on the unspeakable task awaiting her.

"Where's Matt?" she asked, looking at the circled area of sectors two and five on the map Malloy had handed her.

"Sector two."

"Have BP block off this section of the highway," she pointed to the map, "and we'll land there. A night landing in the desert is no fun, and I don't want any evidence disturbed by the air from the blades."

Malloy immediately radioed Jake's instructions ahead, at the same time thinking he couldn't cut the tension between these two women with one of the chopper blades.

"How was Matt doing, Malloy?" Jake asked, as she peered into to the darkness.

Malloy paused to gather his thoughts. When he spoke, his voice was level, laced with the raspy calmness of a man trying to control his emotions.

"Matt and I did time together in Desert Shield and Desert Storm. He was one of the best officers I'd ever served under. Death is no stranger to him; he's seen his fair share." Then his words faltered. "We had all the contingencies covered. Our intel was good. Nobody should have died. Matt tried to stop the blood from spilling out of the kid. He did everything he could, Jake, CPR, all of it. Christ, we had to pull him away. He pounded the hood of his truck until his hands bled. How's he doing?" Malloy just shrugged.

The reverberating rotors and blades were a far-off thud in Cara's mind as the chopper hurtled them through the night toward the border. She had removed her headphones and was only vaguely aware of Jake and Malloy's conversation, hearing them as if through a vacuum, as she stared out the window. The whole day seemed surreal. She was sitting in a helicopter flying to a crime scene. She had made love to McKenzie, then left her to go to Jake. And now Jake was acting like she didn't even exist.

Did I actually kiss her? Did she kiss me back? What was real? When Cara took her place in the chopper, she had watched Jake's spine noticeably stiffen. Her eyes were shot through with silver while the hard coldness from that first day in Nogales had returned to her face.

No, she doesn't want me anywhere near her. Plus, she's furious because I used connections to be here now. What do I expect, she has a job to do. She's been working nonstop on the border murders and now the deaths of Alejandro and the other BP agents. Matt has to be taking this just as hard. How can I blame them for not wanting a civilian nosing where she isn't wanted?

Cara's analytical mind sifted through the events that had carried her to this moment. After Torres had been exonerated in the killings and she had returned to Tucson, the law firm agreed to unofficially follow the progress of the investigation. The situation and impact of negative press and public opinion threatened relations between the Mexico and the United States. Certain factions wanted someone who could judiciously direct the flow of sensitive information if need be and keep them abreast of any potential threats to affairs of state. When all hell had erupted on the border that night, Cara was contacted and directed to go to Nogales as a covert observer representing the United States government.

The tension that radiated off Jake's body was an almost tangible thing, and the silence between the two women was deafening. Cara hazarded a glance toward Jake, who gave her a blank-faced look before turning away. After their rocky start, Jake had gradually lowered the walls of mistrust. Now they were rising between them again, stone by stone.

Damn, I need to talk to her, I need to explain—but it'll have to wait. Cara's thoughts drifted to Alejandro's always smiling face and to Matt with his easy way and confident manner. There was no doubt in her mind. He was in love with Jake, but how did Jake feel about him?

By the time the 4X4 pulled up, the area was swarming with agents representing every known and some not so known agencies of both the U.S. and Mexico. Springing from the back seat, Kalani, with Cara close on her heels, walked toward Jake. The looming eastern glow did nothing to soften the stark reality of why they were all gathered on this desolate piece of desert. Waiting. Waiting for the light of day to add more reality. Kalani wrapped her arms around Jake. They held each other, both women expressing their profound sorrow and sense of loss through their silent connection, each giving in return the comfort they desperately sought.

Cara felt out of place, as if she were intruding on a private moment, watching the shared emotion between the two friends. She looked away toward the lonely figure standing vigil on the rise where a still body lay; her face showed no emotion, but there was an undeniable ache in her heart. Even when her younger brother Stephen was killed she had no one to share her sorrow with, no one to hold her and comfort her. No one to soothe her guilt.

The scrunch of footsteps on gravel caught her attention, and she turned to see Matt approaching from the CSU van. She watched his cold, blue eyes soften as they focused on Jake.

"Oh, Matt, I am so sorry. Alejandro was a good agent and a good friend." Jake stepped toward Matt and put her arms around him. He steeled his emotions and held onto her as he put one hand on the back of her head and drew her to his chest. In a hoarse voice, he finally spoke.

"I'm glad you're here, Jake. Hector and Roberto are dead. So's Josh. And Alejandro—damn kid went and got himself killed. We were shorthanded. I—I never should have left the two of 'em out here alone."

"Stop it, Matt! This isn't your fault." Jake pushed back to look him in the eye. "They were good agents. It wouldn't have made a difference who was out here. From what Malloy filled us in on, this wasn't a kill because our agents were just in their way. They knew BP had multiple areas staked out and used that to their advantage."

Matt ran his hand over his weary face, his eyes drifting across the distance to where the young agent lay, to where the slain young man's brother waited for the first streak of light so he could begin tracking the murdering smugglers. He fixed his eyes on the horizon. "It'll be a long day. I would like to take them in as soon as I can."

With an ache in her throat, Jake held tight to Matt's hand. "Baltazar and Kalani have already started. I'm going to Alejandro now."

Matt resigned himself to Cara's presence and his directive to allow her full access to the investigation. He didn't dislike her. In fact, he had come to admire the tenacious, attractive lawyer, acknowledging her tough and resilient nature, knowing she could handle her own. Turning and walking over to Cara, he stood within inches of her and watched as her brown eyes narrowed. She held her ground as Matt stared directly into her eyes.

"I don't need anyone else out here hurt, and I haven't got the manpower to assign anyone to you, so you're with Jake."

"I can take care of myself, I don't need a baby-sitter," she growled.

Just as Jake opened her mouth to protest, Malloy, who had been standing to the side, thankful he wasn't in the firing line of the other three, handed Jake an envelope. "It's official, Jake, you got her."

She read the paper without comment, then turned on her heels toward Kalani. "Let's go to work."

The sun rode high over the Sonoran Desert as Craig Ochoa tossed a blanket and saddle across the back of his pinto mare. With the patience of his ancestors, the uniformed Apache had lingered on the fringes of the crime scene watching Jake's walk-through. Every time she placed a marker at a point of possible evidence, he felt a minute twitch in the corner of his eye. Other CSI team members methodically processed the scene. One stepped further and further away from Alejandro's body and the main area of action to collect samples of peripheral bloodstains and chart the blood spatter patterns. Another, equipped with Vacutainers, searched for blood trails leading away from the scene. Craig knew the yellow-topped vials meant any collected samples were bound for DNA testing, but he also knew the only blood evidence they would find would come from Alejandro.

His hawk-like eyes darted over the scene to the cold form lying in the dust. CSI was videotaping, photographing, and sketching every inch and documenting it all on a chain of custody forms. The bodies of the slain Border Patrol agents were now crime scenes, he thought. When CSI began moving Alejandro down from the hill to a van for transport back to the morgue in Nogales, Craig rose in silent reverence. He was deep in thought as Matt approached him carrying two mugs of steaming coffee.

"What can you tell me, Craig?"

Craig's eyes hardened as he brought the cup to his mouth. "Alejandro knew the man who killed him. So did Josh." He took a deep breath. The air was thick with the smell of mesquite and creosote. Shifting the toe of his boot in the gravel, Craig continued.

"Josh was the first one to die, a knife through the heart. Then the killer circled around that outcropping there," he pointed, "and made his way to the trail and then up to where Alejandro was positioned."

Here, the sentient Shadow Wolf paused, closed his eyes, and listened. Matt had learned a long time ago not to question what Craig, or any of the Shadow Wolves, knew— or how they knew it. He waited for the dark-skinned man to speak again. When he did, his lightly accented voice was restrained, as unmoving as the rage that enveloped him, as detached as his anguish-filled soul.

"He waited awhile by a clump of creosote bushes before approaching Alejandro from behind. Alejandro stood up, turned to face the man; there was no surprise, no fear. He even shifted his weight a few times as he and the killer talked. Alejandro never drew his pistol. I figure whoever killed him waited until the gunfire started at the other stakeout, then pulled a 9mm. I think he was aiming at Alejandro's head, but the swiveling boot imprint suggests that Alejandro swiped at the gun, knocking it down, deflecting the bullet through his hand and chest. The shooter never went over to check to see if he was dead. He just turned and walked to the top of the hill." Craig tossed his head toward the knoll. "It's the highest point, so he was probably signaling it was clear to cross over with the drugs."

Matt felt his guts clench, his eyes frozen in the image Craig had painted. His mind frantically tried to refute what he was hearing. "Someone he knew? Craig, just before he died, Alejandro was trying to tell me something. I think you might be right. He knew his killer. That would mean...it would have to be—fucking son of a bitch—the only person who could get that close would be—what, a BP agent. And that makes no sense. Or...damn, who the hell else would be out here that time of night that wouldn't spook Alejandro?"

Craig could see the anguish on Matt's face; it mirrored his own. "Judging from the depth of the footprints, the guy weighed about 190 pounds. Favors his left and wears an expensive handmade Mexican boot. There's only a handful of artisans in Mexico could turn out a boot like that. Jake made casts of the heel print—each boot maker has a specific signature, like a brand on the heel."

Craig turned, untied the reins of his horse, and mounted. Matt knew what direction Craig was heading. And why.

"I'll let you know what I find, Matt."

"You're heading to Mexico," Matt stated flatly.

"Yes, my brother."

Craig reached up to remove the badge from his shirt and handed it to Matt.

"Craig..."

"You don't need to say anything."

Matt simply nodded his head in understanding as he pocketed the badge. "If you need anything, *amigo*...anything, you hear?"

Craig straightened, sitting tall in the saddle as he focused on the shrill screech just above him. A single chocolate-brown Harris hawk soared overhead. Again he breathed in the desert and closed his eyes, listening to the spirit voices echoing across the ages just below the keening wind. The sign was unmistakable. He turned his horse toward Mexico, alone.

Dusk was creeping over the mountains, coloring them with indigo shadows when Jake stood and looked out across the desert, her eyes surveying the different colored markers that punctuated the scrub where the illegals had fallen. She thought how simple it all seemed. So neat and tidy, like a board game, a colored flag replacing a once living, breathing human being. She wondered if they would be able to identify the dead to notify next of kin or if anyone would miss them. She stretched her neck from side to side and snapped the rubber gloves from her sweating hands. The last of the dead from both sectors had been transported to a temporary morgue in Nogales. The less seriously wounded went to the hospital in Nogales, while the critical cases were airlifted to Tucson Medical Center.

Daylight waned as Jake observed her crew diligently processing the scene. They worked with unflagging intensity, moving across the site with the expertise of their profession. All had seen death in all its debased forms, but the mindless slaughter of defenseless illegals cut down from behind as they ran for their lives made for a somber task.

Jake worked right alongside her crew and had done so all day without complaint. As she tired, her guard faltered and she found herself focused on Cara. She automatically scanned the throng of technicians. Cara was standing off to the side of the equipment van, looking particularly agitated as she engaged a Border Patrol agent, who was part of the Border Homicide Task Force, in conversation. As much as Jake wanted to harbor her anger with her, she couldn't. However improbable it seemed to her, the sight of the insufferable woman made her heart race, even with her dirt-smudged face and bloodstained clothes.

Just as Jake brought her fingers to her lips, remembering the kiss in the hallway of the hotel, Cara's angst-ridden brown eyes found hers. Jake risked a reserved smile at her. It was infectious, and Cara's lips curved upward in return. At that moment, as the light faded across the desert, everything around them was forgotten. It was just the two of them, each remembering the touch and feel, the essence, of the other.

Kalani's voice interrupted and drew Jake's eyes from Cara.

"I'm sorry, what did you say?"

"We've done what we can for today, it's time to go in," Kalani said again while she lightly rubbed Jake's back.

"Yes, you're right, have our crew meet me in the command tent as soon as they gather their equipment." With a heavy sigh, she talked into the dimming light. "Will we ever stop this curse, Kalani? It's like fighting back a tidal wave, this never-ending flow of drugs and death across the border. Ruthless bastards!"

Kalani squeezed Jake's hand. "All we can do is try, Jacquelyn."

Jake had thanked her crew for their uncomplaining diligence and was loading up her gear when Cara came up behind her. She sensed Cara's presence moments before she heard her tired voice. "Can I get a ride to Ruby's Inn, Jake?"

Jake turned, looked Cara in the eye, then ran her gaze over her ruined suit. "You might as well come to the ranch with me. You haven't eaten all day, and you could use a shower and change of clothes."

She threw the last of her gear in the back of the truck and headed toward the driver's door. "Come on, get in."

The two women shared little conversation on the drive to the ranch house, but each felt a comfort in the presence of the other. The dusk-to-dawn light cast a welcome glow across the porch as Jake pulled into the driveway. She closed her weary eyes and leaned her head against the back of the seat for a moment before looking at Cara.

"You hungry?"

"Not very, but coffee sounds good. What sounds even better is getting out of these clothes and into that shower you offered."

As the two women entered the homey kitchen, the pleasant aroma of food greeted them. Jake's housekeeper always prepared something before she left when Jake worked late. She read the note Juanita had left on the kitchen table.

"Well, looks like we have lasagna and salad." Jake's voice softened as she looked into Cara's weary face. "Hey, why don't you go shower. I'll set things out and pour us a glass of wine."

Cara longed to hold the exhausted-looking blonde, to comfort and be comforted by the woman she had grown to care so much about, but instead kept her distance. "You're just as tired as I am, probably more. Why don't we both go clean up, then we can share that glass of wine?"

Too tired to argue, Jake welcomed the thought of the hot water on her aching body. "Deal. You know where the guestroom is. There are clean towels in the bath and clothes in the dresser. Help yourself."

Cara watched the exhausted doctor walk out of the kitchen, then pushed her own tired body down the hall to the guestroom.

Both women lingered under the pounding hot water of their showers, allowing it to ease their aching muscles, but for Cara nothing lessened the pain and angst of the events of the past day. She could still hear the mournful wailing of the wounded. The cruel reality of the senseless killings made her tense and edgy. Scrubbing the dirt and blood from her hands, the sight launched her back to the last time she felt so alone...so lost.

It was when Stephen, her younger brother, was killed. He'd spun off a hairpin curve, driving too fast after he found Maggie, his lifelong love and fiancée, in his sister's arms.

After the fight, he had stormed out to his car and left. Cara remembered how she had chased after him, desperate to explain what he had seen. Helplessly she saw him lose control in the curve. It was like slow motion, frame after frame, watching the car sail over the cliff, climbing down the treacherous rocks, dragging Stephen from the car before it exploded in flames. Even then it was too late. He had died on impact—a broken neck. She never had the chance to tell him tell him she was sorry.

Maggie, hysterical after Stephen and Cara fought and raced out of the estate, had blurted the story to their grandfather. Sebastian Cipriano had not uttered a word to Cara since then. It was the day her world and all she loved died. Not a day passed since that night that she didn't see Stephen's face and lifeless body in her mind when she was awake or in her dreams when she managed to sleep. Stephen, her baby brother whose adoration bordered on idolization of his sister, was the only soul she had ever loved with all her heart besides her grandfather. Tears mingled with the water running down her body as she sank to the floor of the shower.

Finished with her shower, Jake dressed and went to the kitchen to prepare the meal. After pouring the wine and setting out the dishes, she called to Cara.

"Dinner's ready, Counselor!"

A few moments passed while Jake waited, nibbling at the edges of the casserole. But Cara never appeared. Concerned, Jake went to the guestroom. She tapped lightly on the door and called out Cara's name again, but there was still no answer. Pushing the slightly ajar door open, she stuck her head in. "Cara?"

A muffled noise came from inside, and she crossed the room to listen. The fiasco of the day still gripped her—and it was her job; she could only imagine how it all was affecting

Cara. *I need to check on her,* Jake thought as she heard what sounded like sobbing. Fearing something was wrong, Jake entered the bathroom. She could see Cara through the steamy glass of the shower doors, crouched on the tile floor with her knees drawn up to her chest. Without hesitation, she opened the shower. Quickly turning off the water, she stepped in and knelt down beside her.

"What is it, Cara? Are you all right? Have you been hurt?"

Cara raised her tear-filled eyes to the caring face of the woman she knew she'd fallen in love with.

How could I have ever thought those eyes were cold, Jake wondered, moistness forming in her own eyes in response to the overwhelming pain she saw on Cara's face. As Jake gently touched Cara's cheek and helped her to stand, she felt the slightest tremble and thought the woman was dealing with the trauma of the day's ordeal.

Cara moved her hand over Jake's and held her fingers to her lips, lightly kissing them. A huskiness saturated her voice as her strong arms gathered an unresisting Jake close to her. "Oh Jake, I'm sorry. I just...I...I need you...so much."

Their lips met for the second time in twenty-four hours, but it seemed like a lifetime had passed. Breathlessly, Jake broke the kiss, and she quivered as she felt Cara's naked body against her. No words passed between them as their eyes met. Cara merely brushed a wet strand of hair behind her ear, then raised a finger to Jake's mouth and traced her lips before she leaned toward her. With the warmth of Jake's lips against her own, Cara twined her fingers through blonde hair, pulled her closer, and then kissed down the curve of her jaw.

As Cara tilted Jake's head up and to the side, her exploratory nips on Jake's exposed throat elicited yet another tremor as Jake's heart faltered. Her breathing stopped amid the diverse emotions that gripped her as firmly as the arms holding her. She wrapped her arms around Cara's neck and fell wholly into the embrace. Suddenly able to breathe again, she pressed against the supple body that was so close, but not close enough.

"It's been so long since I've felt anything like that," Jake whispered.

Cara nodded in agreement, but Jake simply turned and left the bathroom. Snagging a towel from the rack, uncertainty filling her breast, Cara followed, coming to stand behind Jake in the bedroom. She hesitated a moment before placing a hand on Jake's waist. "Now it's my turn to ask if you're okay."

In one fluid movement, Jake turned around and into Cara's arms. "Yes, I'm more than okay."

And with that, Cara continued to explore receptive lips, holding Jake more gently than she had ever known she could hold a woman. When she loosened her arms to run her hands through Jake's hair, their eyes met, and irrepressible urges took over. Caresses along Jake's mouth and down her neck resonated with the escalating passions of a heart that had been too long isolated.

Jake answered every touch of Cara's lips, clenching her fingers through wet chestnut hair and holding her tighter. Her breathing had improved to small gasps only to be stolen again when Cara's tongue glided smoothly across her teeth to her tongue. That kiss, a benediction unto itself, composed answers to questions she didn't even know she had, unexpected answers that started somewhere near her left breast and spiraled downward to an increasingly warm moistness.

Cara broke the kiss to delicately trail her lips down an elegant neck, letting her tongue taste Jake's heat, feel the pulsing rhythm just beneath her skin. Tenderly, her hands drifted across the smaller woman's back, easing down to momentarily clasp the gently curved buttocks before coming back to bring her closer and ease them both onto the bed.

Jake could feel the thudding of Cara's heart matching her own as they lay embraced on the smooth sheets. She threw her head back and exposed her neck to more of the soft nibbles and caresses, feeling the welcome press of one well-muscled leg slide across both of her own. She was overwhelmed with sensations as butterfly touches fluttered over her shoulders while her own hands explored Cara's sculpted thigh, now so very near.

Both lovers were breathing faster. Emotions long hidden surfaced from inside each heart. Pent-up passions, provoked by both women's glimpse into the finality of death, released in a single moment of trust and understanding.

"Cara, I..." Jake started, her voice breaking slightly, not knowing exactly what she wanted to say, at a loss as to how to express what she wanted.

"It's all right," Cara soothed in a breathy whisper as she brought her mouth back up to part the questioning lips gently with the tip of her tongue. Her hands reached to hold the sides of the flushed face below her, and her heart beat even more rapidly. Drawing long fingers easily across slender shoulders, down sinuous arms to the edge of the offending shirt that still separated them, Cara pushed her hands underneath to brush skin so velvety soft that her hand trembled at the sensation. She could feel the tremors rising from Jake's body, too, as she undressed her, exposing the smooth lines of her body. Baring her breasts to the rarified night air, then cupping them in both hands, she nestled her head between them, inhaled deeply, and then lay there a moment, listening to the surging lifeblood mimic a thundering storm.

Jake brought her arms up and about Cara's dark head, holding the other woman to her breast, lovingly caressing her cheek. Cara sensed the hesitancy in that touch and raised her head to meet Jake's eyes, eyes that were unsure of what came next, what might be welcome.

Grinning slightly, one corner of her mouth lifted, she covered Jake's hands with her own and placed them on her breasts. Jake gasped at the sight of Cara's taut nipples and uplifted breasts within reach of her lips. The sight was too much, and with unabashed fascination, she quickly took advantage of it. Smoothing her hands around the silken flesh of both breasts, she lifted them closer and slipped her mouth over two pebbled nipples. Her heart surged at the intimacy. She felt and heard Cara catch her breath as she teased each nipple with her tongue. But in the next second, Jake lost her breath and her mind swayed as a knee strategically slipped between her legs.

Cara poured her heart and soul into each caress. She was conscious of every breath, of every tremor, of every gasp that coursed through Jake's body. Captivated by the emotions, she committed herself entirely to showing her how much she meant to her. Murmuring reassuring words, she leaned forward, her long hair brushing softly over sensitive skin, to release kisses onto the lids of hazel eyes, to nibble on a bottom lip, to suckle swollen breasts. Cara slid her hands under Jake, and lifting her hips to pull the delicate material slowly down, she revealed golden curls glistening with wetness.

"Oh...Cara...please..." Jake gasped, reaching for the other woman.

"Shh...let me...let me show..." Cara heard her own breathless voice mingled with Jake's as she gently pushed the hungering arms aside, one leg fully parting Jake's thighs as she meshed their bodies together in a sensual embrace. Taking her time, Cara slipped down the length of her and rested her head just below Jake's navel. With her body stretched between opened legs, she felt Jake's hands, the soft fingers teasing their way across her shoulders. And her own arms came around the outside of the other woman's hips, gripping them harder in anticipation. She breathed in the scents of Jake's growing expectation as she ran her tongue lightly along the inside cleft of first one leg, then the other.

Jake hungrily gripped Cara's head and tangled her hands through her hair as the pressure built within, an instinctive desire that could not be denied. She heard herself make a tiny whimpering noise as Cara lowered her mouth closer, her breath teasing her, seducing her. Jake's heart echoed in her throat as she tried to contain what she could not. Completely powerless, as vulnerable as she'd ever been in her life, she gave herself to this woman.

Cara paused to inhale more deeply, savoring, as she moved her hands beneath Jake and raised her to her lips. She felt the strong, trembling legs wrap around her shoulders, heard the first whimpering cries that came when her tongue slowly entered. At that moment, with every touch, Cara put her entire being into bringing Jake the purest of pleasures.

Intense swells of rhythmic contractions rose inside Jake with each warm touch of Cara's tongue. Her back arched hard, and she cried out as the brilliant wave of white light flashed behind her eyes. Her body convulsed, and she heard a sound like rushing water as her vision dimmed. It seemed to last forever, and she never wanted it to end. For just a moment, it seemed that she would surely die.

As the intensity of the orgasm gradually ebbed and reality started edging back in, Jake's heart swelled and she was compelled to pull Cara up to her. And so she did, with an eagerness that surprised them both, to meet her anticipating lips. She raised her head to see the most beautiful warm brown eyes. In wonder, she gazed at the single tear streaking down Cara's cheek.

Jake touched the tear track in awe, fully aware of its meaning, and as simple as that, there were no more doubts of the love that she saw shining on her at that moment. She gently coaxed Cara up toward her and cradled Cara's head to rest on her breast, knowing that it was only a beginning. Her lips pressed against Cara's forehead briefly. Soon she would

give as much pleasure to this beloved woman's spirit and
body as she herself had been given.

Chapter Ten

Craig Ochoa traced a symbol in the white sand as he crouched against the crumbling adobe wall of the humble dwelling on the outskirts of the small seaport city of Guaymas, Sonora.

"Is this your mark, *señor*?"

Never acknowledging Craig's presence, the *peón*, with his callused hands, methodically worked the boot leather stretched across the last. Respectfully, Craig remained silent until the elderly man wiped his hands across his apron and wordlessly ambled inside his shop. He returned to the shaded work area with a pair of exquisitely hand-crafted leather boots. Still without a word, he placed the boots on a crude wooden table, moved back to his bench, and continued to stretch and shape the rich, chocolate leather, releasing its earthy scent into the air.

The tracker picked up one of the boots. Turning it over, he traced the intricate detailing. Finally focusing on the heel, he ran his fingers over the markings as if reading Braille.

"How much do you want, *amigo*, for this fine boot?"

The man stopped and gazed out with rheumy eyes toward the Sea of Cortez, to the rise and fall of the azure, white-capped surf as, with tireless persistence, it claimed the sands then retreated into itself.

"The man, *señor*, who ordered these boots did not like them, so I will give you a good price."

As Craig reached into his shirt pocket for the money, the bootmaker's elderly brown eyes went to the grey feather pinned there. The old man shook his head.

"No, my friend. You take the boots. I will be proud for the Shadow Wolf to wear them. If they serve you well, you come back and pay, *sí?*"

The two men had never met or spoken before, yet the old bootmaker knew this man of the grey feather would come. A knowing look passed between them. Craig stood now shoulder to shoulder with the wizened old man. His eyes, too, focused out toward the sea—seeking, questioning.

"The man who did not want the boots, shall I tell him you are making another pair?"

"*Sí*, it would be good to tell him I am making him a special pair. They will soon be finished."

"Where can I find this man, *señor?*"

Years of life with all its travails lay etched upon his weathered face and gnarled hands. Craig discerned no fear in the faded eyes that now focused on a picture hanging on the cracked adobe wall that supported the makeshift roof of the work area. What he saw was a man who had lived his life and was at peace...waiting.

"The woman in the picture, she is lovely, my friend."

The old man gently brushed the dust from the picture. "*Sí*, my Lupita, she was the most beautiful." He paused a moment to catch his labored breath. "I am a simple man, *señor*. My Lupita and I lived on this piece of earth here by the blue waters for fifty years. She is gone now, and I will join her soon. The evil cannot hurt her now."

Silence, punctuated only by the occasional gull squawk, pervaded as the bootmaker's eyes turned reflective. "There is a place outside Santa Ana, it is not a good place, one must be very careful. He is known only as *La Serpiente*. He wears the uniform of the Federales."

Craig never flinched as his eyes gazed out across the horizon, to that obscure line where the blue of the sky met the blue of the sea. "I will tell him about the boots, my friend."

As Craig walked toward the battered pickup, he heard the man say, "Your brother, he was a good man. Be watchful, Shadow Wolf. You go where evil lives."

Winding his way up Route 15 from Guaymas to Hermosillo, then on to Imuris where he had left his horse and borrowed his cousin's truck, Craig tried to shuffle the pieces into place. He was not surprised the man he was looking for was Mexican police. Mexico had long been plagued with corrupt law enforcement and politicians. What bothered him was the fog-shrouded figure lurking in the shadows of his thoughts. He had long heard the name *La Serpiente*, cursed and whispered in fear upon the wind, blowing like dust across the desert. It gnawed and twisted in his gut that this man walked amongst them and wore two faces.

As he neared Imuris, he realized it all made sense—all the times the drug runners seemed to be one step ahead of them, always eluding even the newest checkpoints, changing routes at the last minute and avoiding arrest, flooding the States with their poison, scarring the land and leaving a trail of broken dreams and murder. It all came clear in his mind how it was that his brother had allowed his murderer to walk within two feet of him and shoot him point-blank.

Matt sat at Alejandro's desk, a cardboard box in front of him. In his hand was the last thing to pack away, a pack of cinnamon gum. He half expected to hear Alejandro say, "You want a piece, boss?" *Damn kid, his jaw was always chewing gum.* Everything else had been packed to deliver to Alejandro's family, but he couldn't bring himself to give up this last reminder of his friend. He slipped the gum into his shirt pocket.

Most of the day passed as Matt remained in the workroom next to his office, a half-empty bottle of tequila añejo on the desk in front of him. On one side of the room were the photographs of the scenes where his agents and the illegals had been ambushed, and on the other side were the gruesome pictures of the Jane Doe murder scenes. His eyes burned from looking at the images, but he forced himself to focus. They had buried four agents that day, and he was worried that he hadn't heard from Craig since he'd gone into Mexico three days ago. He hadn't seen much of Jake either. He missed her. Every time he did try to spend time with her, she was too busy. Matt thought she was avoiding him, still mad as hell because she had to lead Vittore around. Both women had attended the task force meetings every day but spoke very little to each other and even less to him.

He poured himself another *caballito* of tequila as he looked at a picture of the boot prints of the man who killed Alejandro, hoping each little pony of the pure agave añejo would numb his thoughts and kill the bitter taste in his mouth that was hard to swallow—the fact that Alejandro knew and trusted the person who had killed him.

Suddenly, Matt bolted from his chair and slammed the glass down on the desk with such force that the bottle fell to the floor and shattered. He was breathing shallow and fast, his bloodshot eyes squinting as he tore the picture of the boot print off the board and compared it to the ones they'd been lucky to recover at the murder scene of the last Jane Doe. He rubbed his eyes as if trying to clear them.

"I'll be goddamned! It's the same boot, the same fucking boot!"

Just as he was about to pick up the phone to call Jake, a shadow fell across the doorway.

"That's a damn waste of good tequila, Matt," Craig said matter-of-factly, looking at the broken glass on the floor.

Relief washed over Matt's angst-ridden, rugged face. "'Bout time you showed up."

A moment of silence passed between the two men. Finally Matt broached the subject. "We had services today for Josh, Hector, Roberto. And Alejandro."

"I know, my friend. Alejandro came to me in a vision last night. He walks with the ancient ones, but his spirit does not rest."

Craig looked at the picture in Matt's hands. "We have much to talk of, but first, let's go get stinking drunk."

Cara sat on the veranda, lit only by the illuminate glow of a full moon, looking up at the night sky. The air was bursting with nocturnal sounds—coyotes howling in the distance, the gruntings of javelina foraging through the mesquite in their hunt for water and succulent prickly pear. The desert at night was alive and bustling with activity, ironically mirroring the hectic pace of the past few days with the task force meetings full of unwelcome looks and the meetings with Mexican officials who smiled politely, denied any wrongdoing on the part of Mexico and then asked how much the U.S. would compensate them for the inconvenience to their citizens. It all had been harrowing, to say the least. In spite of it all, however, Cara felt alive. The void in her heart that had been her constant companion since Stephen's death now brimmed over with an incomparable warmth.

Her thoughts floated to Jake and the incredible sensation of their lovemaking. *Making love doesn't even come close to how I felt about that night,* she thought. She remembered how her heart had quivered all night with Jake curled in her arms and how when the sun cast its beams across the bed she knew she had never felt the way she did just then. Touching Jake, breathing her in, calmed her restless soul, yet it terrified her at the same time. Opening her heart, allowing Jake to touch the rawness, petrified her, but it frightened her more to think she could have lived her life without ever knowing her. Cara knew that in the joining of their hearts, they were bound forever.

A voice as soft as the night air interrupted her pondering. "We need to quit meeting like this, Counselor."

Cara turned to see Jake bathed in ribbons of moonlight, standing in her bare feet and sleep shirt that came to the top of her long sculpted legs. Her breath caught in her chest at the overwhelming loveliness of the sight of the woman who held her heart.

With a voice equally as soft, she asked, "Hey, did you sleep well? Hungry? Juanita left fried chicken."

Jake moved smoothly over to Cara and straddled her hips, tucking her face into her neck. "Thank you for letting me sleep and," with a suggestive chuckle, "other things."

Cara slipped her hands under Jake's sleep shirt to the exquisite softness of her skin, pulling her closer. "You're more than welcome," she murmured as her lips grazed the pulse point of Jake's neck. "It was my pleasure."

"Hmm," Jake said, tracing Cara's lips with her tongue, "if I recall, I fell asleep before I could reciprocate."

Opening her mouth to the offered tongue, she ever so gently drew the warmth in, whispering between feather kisses, "Do you think...all night...will do?"

Jake's heart was pounding out of her chest, her desire burning along every nerve ending, every fiber of her being. Cara made her crazy, crazy with the need to possess. With all inhibition gone, the passion and desire to bring to her every pleasure she had received was all consuming. Her voice filled with passion.

"Cara, I want you, let me make love to you, please let me love you."

Matt brought his hand to his mouth, licking off the salt before tossing back the shot of tequila. "The old man said we might find this *La Serpiente* around Santa Ana. Do you trust him?"

Craig mimicked Matt's actions before sucking on a lime. "The old man spoke the truth of the dying. He spoke with an honest tongue, without fear."

The two lawmen matched shot for shot, downing the amber liquid of the agave plant, but their eyes and senses remained clear and sharp as they traded information.

"You brought the boots back with you?"

"In the truck. I'll drop 'em by your office tomorrow. It's not only the identifying mark on the heel, Matt. The skill and distinct tooling of the leather are unique. They'd be easy to spot, no doubt about it."

Matt leaned back in his chair, the purest expression of hate drawn on his face. "I have some time off coming, you up to another trip back into Mexico, my friend?"

Craig knew crossing the border to track the ruthless killer could cost both of them their badges. Rubbing his chin, his eyes narrowing, he threw the shot glass on the rough floor of the cantina, then ground it with purpose under the heel of his boot.

"I haven't taken a vacation in a long time, it's 'bout time."

The two men continued to drink until the barkeep started to put the chairs on top of the tables. Matt got up, apologized, then threw a handful of bills on the table.

As the tracker and the lawman walked into the uncertainty of the night, Matt stopped and reached into his shirt pocket. "This belongs to you."

Craig closed his large hand over the shiny badge and clipped it to his shirt. "I'll see you in the morning, Matt."

It seemed she had just fallen asleep, limbs intertwined with Cara's, holding her protectively to her breast with arms around her waist, when Jake woke to the pounding on the door of the ranch house. She cocked her head to listen, trying not to wake Cara. *Maybe I dreamt it.* Not hearing anything, she laid her cheek against the soft swell of Cara's breast, inhaling her musky caramel scent. It filled her senses, arousing her yet again. Her tongue had a mind of its own as it sought the dark nipple and began to trace the outline of the perfect nub. Cara moaned as her nipple hardened in response to Jake's attention. Still asleep, her hands moved down to cup Jake's buttocks while her thigh slid up between Jake's legs. Just as Jake gently closed her teeth on the delicacy in her mouth, the pounding at the door came again, causing her to jerk abruptly away from Cara, waking her. Alarmed, she jumped up and grabbed her robe.

"Who in the hell can that be at this hour?" She looked back into sleepy, questioning eyes.

"I think I like being awakened the other way. Do you want me to get up and come with you or go into the guestroom?"

Jake hesitated a moment. "No, it's okay, try to go back to sleep. I'll see who it is."

Jake padded down the hall to the entryway, tying her robe around her nakedness as she went. She flipped on the porch light, looking through the peephole to see Matt standing there. When she opened the door, her concern threatened to turn to anger when the distinctive and overpowering smell of tequila assaulted her nostrils. But Matt wasn't normally a drinker. She stayed her irritation, realizing he was trying to cope with the death of four agents under his command. It had thrown him more than he showed. To most, but not Jake, he seemed to be holding up.

Folding her arms across her chest, she looked into his cloudy blue eyes. "You want to come in, Matt?"

He wobbled into the kitchen with her. "Sorry 'bout it being so late, Jake, but I need to talk to you."

"Sit down. Looks to me what you need is some coffee."

Matt smiled sheepishly. "Sounds good. We need to go over a few things."

"Mind if I join you?"

Both Matt and Jake turned to see a curious, sleep shirt and jean-clad Cara standing barefoot in the doorway. Jake pulled her robe tighter around her body as a rush of warmth washed over her. Her eyes traveled the length of the stunning woman in the doorway as she muttered, "Excuse me, just let me get some clothes on," then brushed passed Cara, hurrying down the hall.

After a pot of strong coffee, Matt ran down all he and Craig had discovered. He knew they had found a link that could lead them to not only the sadistic killer of the young Hispanic women but the cowardly drug runner and murderer of Alejandro and the rest of his men as well.

"Jesus, Matt. You know you can't go into Mexico officially. If you and Craig do, you both can lose your jobs!" She slammed her fist on the counter. "For two cents, I'd go with you myself if I wouldn't stick out like a sore thumb!" Jake rambled on in excitement. "If this guy is as feared as you say, your lives aren't going to be worth much down there, asking questions."

Matt watched the green fire arcing from Jake's eyes downward to every muscle of her body. He had thought it impossible that she could be any more beautiful, but at that moment she was. He wanted her to be his wife and share their life, raise a family. He would wait until he came back, but then it was time to find out if she felt the same way.

"I figure if we can connect with the *coyotes*, they can lead us to their boss. The only thing is they will run scared, and you're right, no one will want to answer questions, but we have to go, Jake."

An edge of frustration creep into Jake's voice. "Damn, Matt, isn't there any other way to flush this bastard out?"

Startled, both Jake and Matt stared blankly at Cara when they heard her say, "I might have an idea."

Jake jumped up from the chair, knocking it to the floor, her body straining with tension and disbelief after hearing Cara's plan. Her face reddened.

"You—you will not go down there! That is the craziest plan I've ever heard! You could be hurt. God damn it, Cara, you could be killed!" She threw her cup into the sink. "This isn't a game for goddamn amateurs! No way, forget it!"

Cara opened her mouth to protest, but Matt interrupted first. "She's right, but..." He rubbed his chin in thought. "It could work if we stayed close out of sight. You say this Torres guy would be willing to help?"

"I've talked to him, and he said yes without question. He would pose as my brother and make the contact with the *coyote* in Santa Ana, offer to do whatever it takes to get the ride, even run the drugs if it would get us across. I would be the perfect target for our killer since I have the coloring and the look he seems to go for."

Jake couldn't believe what she was hearing. "Are you two out of your minds? I won't hear another word of this!" She swung around furiously to face both Matt and Cara. "Offer to do whatever is necessary! Do you know what could happen to you down there? Has it occurred to you that you just might have to speak Spanish, for God's sake?"

"You never asked me if I could speak Spanish, which I can and have since I was three years old," Cara replied calmly. "It isn't your decision, Jake, it's mine."

Matt knew there would be no reasoning with Jake that night; her mind was set. "Uh...I guess I better go. Let's sleep on this, and we can go over it in the morning."

Jake's voice was cold and hard as she turned toward the hallway. "There's nothing to talk about. It isn't going to happen. I'm going to bed. You can let yourself out, Matt."

Cara locked up and turned the lights out after Matt left, all the while replaying the heated discussion with Jake. She paused at Jake's bedroom, leaning her head against the closed door a moment, torn as to whether or not to go in and talk to her. Reasonably, she knew Jake needed time, but in her heart she knew she needed Jake. She didn't want to spend what was left of that night or any other night away from her. *Jake, please understand, I need to do this. I need to go to Mexico to try to stop this butcher. So many lives have been lost. We owe it to the ones we can save.* She reached for the doorknob but stopped, not wanting to know if it was locked, then continued down the hall to the guestroom.

Chapter Eleven

Faint glimmerings of dawn were barely creeping into the guestroom when Cara heard the 4x4 pull out of the driveway. From her bed, she had a clear view across the shared courtyard to Jake's room. There had been neither movement nor light to indicate the doctor was up, only the roar of the engine signaling her hasty departure.

A pang of regret followed by a sudden emptiness in the pit of her stomach hit her as she realized the implications. Cara had lain awake most of the night and early morning with the previous night's scene playing over and over in her mind. Jake's voice, light and teasing from earlier in the evening, had grown dark and angry as the argument had progressed. She was angrier than Cara had thought. Cara regretted not going back to Jake's room after Matt had left, that they had allowed the disagreement to keep them in separate rooms. She had stood outside Jake's door, wanting to go in. She wanted to talk to her, wanted to explain why she had to do what had to be done. Most of all though, she wanted Jake to know that she really did care. She wanted her to know the truth. But she had been unable to get past the closed doors of the bedroom or those of her own mind. She hadn't even tried. Instead, she had simply returned to the guestroom, missing the fiery doctor as soon as she had sequestered herself alone in her bedroom.

And that morning, she missed having Jake in her arms when the sun came up. Cara was agitated with herself and disappointed that Jake hadn't told her she was leaving. She lay thinking about all the cold places that lurked inside her soul—places that now knew the warmth of Jake filling them completely. She no longer had the luxury of hiding behind the emotional walls of isolation. Laying her head back on the pillow, she missed Jake more than she thought possible.

"I can't stop you and Craig from going into Mexico, Matt, and I understand why you have to go. But I damn well cannot and will not condone the sheer stupidity of you, even for a second, entertaining this ridiculous idea of allowing Cara to be part of it—to put herself in harm's way as bait! I won't allow it!"

Up to that point, Matt had been calmly sitting at his desk with his feet propped up on the corner of a pulled-out drawer. Jake's ultimatum sent him into a flurry of motion as he swung his legs to the floor and slammed the drawer shut.

"You won't allow it?" he yelled. "Last time I looked, Cara was a big girl capable of making decisions for herself. She's willing to try this, Jake, and I for one admire her for it. If we don't do something, for Christ's sake, more will die, all because of an invisible line in the sand. Their deaths will have been for nothing. Alejandro and Josh deserve more than that, they all do. It's gotta be done, and she's the right one to go in down there and help us flush out this butchering bastard."

As Jake paced back and forth across the room, her entire body shuddered at the thought of Cara being anywhere near the dangers the plan posed. "I don't want to hear any more. This is not going to happen, Matt. You hear me? It's just not going to happen this way. You saw what those women looked like. It's unthinkable to even imagine what they went through as they were dying."

Matt could feel the heat of her fear. She wasn't thinking objectively as an FBI agent, which confused him. "This is more than a job. It's always been personal, but when he killed Alejandro, he made it family. I know you feel the same way, and I know you wouldn't hesitate to go over there with us. I do understand why you are so against this, Jake. I won't deny how dangerous this can be. And I know you and Cara have gotten to be friends, but you seem to be forgetting something."

"And what would that be?" she asked.

"Vittore's a resourceful woman and can damn well take care of herself. If she could just flush out the connection in Santa Ana, it might get us closer to nailing this killer. You know the Mexican government hasn't officially asked for the FBI's help— guess murdering their young women isn't considered a violation of their civil rights. Hell, these poor, desperate women mean nothing to their government, dead or alive. And BP damn well doesn't have the authority to officially go in there either."

Matt stepped nearer and took Jake's hands gently within his grip. He saw the anguish and frustration and knew that no matter how much he rationalized, Jake was right. It would be dangerous for Cara. "You know she could do it, Jake. Those brown eyes of hers could seduce a saint—and she speaks Spanish."

"Yeah, well, saints are dead, so where does that put her if she's seducing them?"

She could feel the bristle of jealousy edging into her voice as he expressed how beautiful Cara was...and the fact that he noticed. Confused emotions surged through her. Was she jealous because Matt thought Cara was a desirable woman or because he thought the woman that had become her lover was desirable? She was trying to stay focused on what Matt was saying, but her thoughts were on Cara. She kicked herself for stomping off to bed alone last night after yelling at her and more so for not going to her. Remembering their lovemaking and how good and right it seemed softened her anger. She had felt uneasy leaving the ranch without speaking to or seeing Cara that morning.

I never learn from my mistakes. Sam and I had a fight the morning he died. He wanted to talk about our future, about the marriage, for weeks, and I put him off because I wasn't sure it was what I wanted. He deserved better, and I refused to talk that morning he borrowed my car and was blown to pieces in my place. Oh God, what would I do if I lost her now. I've never felt anything like I do when I am with her.

She listened to Matt and Craig outline their plan, but her mind was definitely on her lover.

The golden glow of late afternoon fell across the stack of papers Jake was attempting to sort through. She tapped the pencil repeatedly on her desk, finding it more difficult to concentrate as the day wore on. She hadn't heard from Cara all day, and her own busy schedule hadn't allowed her a minute's break. Flipping open her cell phone, she pulled up Cara's number, but hesitated before pressing the send button. She closed her eyes. *The fight last night, and then I had to go and shut her out. I have no idea what to say.* Jake sighed, forced her eyes open, and pressed send. Cara answered on the second ring. Jake hesitated a moment then her words blurted out in a rush.

"Sorry. Please let me say this. I reacted the way I did because I...I couldn't deal with the thought of you getting hurt or killed. Try to understand, Cara, please. Matt and Craig are law enforcement officers, used to dealing with the scum of the earth. Mexico is not a place you want to be, especially posing as a wanna-be illegal." Jake blushed. "Especially looking the way you do."

Pausing a moment, then softening her voice, Jake asked, "Can we talk about this later? I missed you last night and all day."

"I missed you too, it made me crazy not being next to you. I just didn't know...I've—I borrowed Juanita's truck, and I'm on my way into town to see Matt. Can we go somewhere for dinner...after?"

Jake swallowed her objection and fear. "Come to my office. We can stop at La Casita in Rio Rico. The food's pretty good, and the salsa's hot. Or we could just pick up a couple of steaks, cook them over the pit at the ranch? We already have fresh bread and salad makings."

"I'd rather be alone with you, so I vote for the steaks. See you in a bit."

The aroma of steak sizzling over mesquite wood permeated the evening air as Cara stood at the kitchen sink washing vegetables for a salad. Sipping on a glass of wine, she looked out the open window at Jake tending to the steaks on the grill. Jake's hair was tied loosely back, but the wind occasionally lifted a few wisps as it made the cottonwoods rustle. The light cotton, thigh-length shirt she wore over her two-piece swimsuit moved gently across her body and outlined her slender figure. Jake often took a late night swim; she said it always relaxed her after a day's work. Cara smiled as her body warmed, remembering the passionate lovemaking after she'd slipped into the cool water to join her when they had gotten to the ranch a few hours earlier.

Quietly stepping onto the patio, Cara eased behind Jake and slipped her arms around her. "Hey, the salad and bread's ready. How about your end of the deal? Those steaks done yet?"

"Just give them about two minutes more and we'll be ready. Do we have wine?"

"Do we have wine."

"That's a simple yes or no answer, Counselor. I don't need a full deposition here," Jake interrupted laughingly.

"Yes."

"Good."

"Let's eat, then."

Both women laughed as they moved the food to the patio table and continued to talk and tease each other throughout the meal. After finishing and clearing away the dishes, they pulled their chairs together by the pool and gathered in the night air, gazing at the impossibly bright stars that dotted the sky endlessly. Without warning, Jake moved into the chaise lounge with Cara.

"And what do you want?" Cara asked coyly.

"Just you," Jake whispered, no longer taunted by her doubts and confusion over her feelings. They settled into a comfortable embrace. After a few moments, Jake shifted slightly in Cara's arms.

"I'm sorry," she said softly, knowing that she had caused Cara pain by her abrupt departure and absence.

"Doesn't matter, I understand," Cara said, her lips brushing against Jake's temple.

After a long silence, Jake prompted, "Tell me what you're thinking?"

"Regrets," Cara replied honestly.

Jake turned in Cara's arms to look at her. "Regrets? About what?" she asked, grateful that they were together, sharing such closeness, such intimacy. The time apart had been unbearable.

Cara considered her words carefully. "I regret many things I've done, things I have to live with. And I regret the years I've missed loving you."

Jake stroked the side of Cara's cheek. "Or that after this insane idea of you going undercover in Mexico...that there might not be any more time." Then she fell silent, waiting for Cara's response.

"I should have told you how I feel about you before now. I should have come to you last night."

Jake closed her eyes, wishing she could block out the pain that shimmered in Cara's voice. "I'm listening now," she told her.

Cara felt her throat tighten as tears pricked her eyes. She blinked, then swallowed hard, forcing down a lump so that she could speak.

"I think I knew from the start," she said softly. "When I walked into Maria's that day and saw you sitting at the counter with powdered sugar on your face, staring at me as if I were the one making a fool of myself, I knew you were full of the devil and there'd be hell to pay. And I remember thinking that nobody ever mentioned that the devil was so beautiful." Cara paused as she felt Jake's arms tighten about her. "Soon after, once you let me past that tough exterior, I realized that it didn't matter how angry you planned on staying. I wasn't going to let you push me away or hide. And now it's all about truth."

Jake stroked her hair in a comforting gesture, knowing that it was difficult for Cara to tell her these truths. "Shh," she whispered, and she felt Cara's body relax as the anxiety faded. Swallowing against the dryness in her throat, Jake implored, "Tell me the truth now, Cara."

"The simple truth is, I love you, Jake," Cara whispered.

Jake didn't answer for a time. Her own heart, so long stilled by the pains of loss, beat fresh with emotions that choked her. Finally, she found her voice. "I know that, because I can feel it."

And she could feel it, in every breath that they seemed to share. Jake turned so that she could see Cara's face, reaching out to touch her cheek. She saw the battle within.

"It's okay," Cara told her. "I'm not going anywhere."

"You could die down there."

"Yes, I could. But I'm not going to."

"You don't know that."

"I have to, Jake. I can't believe that for so long I have carried the emptiness, lived so alone inside myself only to find you and then have it all snatched away. I can't think that way. I have to believe that nothing's going to happen except we catch a killer."

"Believe me, it happens, Cara. Please don't go. Don't do this. Don't," Jake begged, her eyes filling with tears. "For some reason, I think that we both are being given another chance here, now with each other. I can't bear to think of losing this."

"We're not going to lose it, Jake. Understand?"

Jake wiped her eyes clear of tears as she stared up at the stars. A faint whisper made its way to Cara. "I promised myself after Sam that I'd never do this again."

Not fully comprehending, Cara asked, "Do what?"

Leveling her eyes at Cara, Jake leaned over to silence her with a kiss. She combed her fingers through Cara's hair, and then calmly proceeded to break her promise.

"I love you, Cara."

In the dark, Cara listened to Jake's breathing as she slept, her chest rhythmically rising and falling beneath her cheek. A slight breeze from the open window disturbed the stillness of the night, carrying the sound of jingling wind chimes as it cooled her skin, still damp with sweat. She slipped out of bed and padded over to the windows, picking up the fallen sheet and wrapping it around her as she stepped out onto the courtyard into a world silvered by the rising moon. She wondered what the day would bring as she watched clouds move in, sailing across the moon like ships.

Turning back to look at her lover, she knew the attraction was more powerful than any she had ever experienced. Jake had opened her heart again. And now she had willingly offered it to her. Easing into bed beside Jake, Cara lifted her damp hair and kissed the side of her face. Jake sighed deeply, taking Cara's hand in her own and kissing it before placing it on her breast. Her tenderness and passion told Cara far more than words as she allowed Jake to pull her closer. They both knew that in a few hours the reality of the undercover mission would come crashing in. But for now, they simply lay entwined in a tender embrace as the rising moon paled behind red-streaked clouds.

Tension radiated through the air as Cara entered the conference room. Craig was there, sitting at the end of the table. Torres was there as well, and Jake was standing by the window. The moment that Cara was seated, Matt came in and laid out the plan.

"What happens after we go across?" Cara asked moments later.

Jake turned a sharp eye on Cara but found that she could not muster her anger. All she felt was fear, fear that Cara could be raped, beaten, or even murdered if they carried through with the plan. Her cycs softened as she took in the inner beauty of the woman she had fallen in love with.

"We have information on the Serpent from undercover ops we've had in place for several weeks in Naco, Hermosillo, and Nogales, Sonora," Matt explained. "After you get to the El Cid Hotel, Torres makes contact with the bartender, tells him he's there to meet with *Los Gatos*. Then you and Torres just wait to be contacted. Intelligence reports indicate that after you make contact with whoever *Los Gatos* is, one of the contacts will get you to the transport location that will then hook up with one of *La Serpiente's* men."

The more they talked, the more Jake felt that familiar apprehension, almost a premonition. It was the same gut-wrenching awareness she got each time a body was found in the desert. She could feel icy fingers clawing at her senses as the sensation closed in on her, and she needed to get out of the room.

"I can see there's no changing your minds on this," Jake interjected. "This is suicide, and you know it."

"Jake, please try to understand. Matt and Craig will be there to watch our backs. We'll have the best transmitters money can buy. It's the only way, and it will work," Cara pled.

Matt did not miss the look that passed between Jake and Cara, and it roused his curiosity. He was aware that it nagged him, but at the same time, he was unaware of why.

"It's just too dangerous. Can't we find another way?" Jake implored.

Matt walked around to Jake, and put his hand on her elbow. She immediately pulled away. Although he didn't know why, he was irritated and his voice showed it.

"Jake, there certainly is another way. We wait. And wait some more. Until we find another dead girl or two or three. And we can do this by the book, not that the Mexican government with their Napoleanic code would know anything about going by the book as we know it. Or that the labyrinth of a justice system we have to deal with will ever get anything done either. But we can do it that way, the sanctioned way."

Matt sat heavily back into his chair. Then in his frustration, he snapped, "You better get your morgue ready and put all your forensic teams on standby. Because the bodies are not going to stop piling up."

It was her eyes that first relented to the truth as he spoke. She knew he was right, but her fear, the thought of losing Cara, was stifling her. Locking eyes with Cara, she knew she couldn't stay in the room any longer. Her heart told her to plead, beg, do anything to keep Cara safe, but her head knew that it was useless to even try.

"I'm sorry," Jake murmured in a quiet voice as she picked up her briefcase and left the room.

Seconds ticked by. A flicker of uncertainty crossed Matt's face as he glared at the door and then at Cara. "She has to be the most impossible woman I know!" he shouted as he began pacing.

Cara just looked away, knowing why Jake was so emotional about her being part of such a dangerous mission—and suddenly aware of Matt's utter confusion.

Regaining his composure, Matt continued with the briefing. After almost an hour, they were set to head out for Santa Ana. He felt confident in Cara's ability to pull it off. "Luckily for us, Cara, you have a handle on how to act your part. Follow Angel's lead."

Matt gestured to Cara's Gucci gold watch. "The clothes will work, but the watch has got to go. Remember, this guy's entire operation has eyes everywhere. Play the part, Cara, you and Torres will have to stay at one of the fleabag hotels in town until the passage is accepted." Directing his attention fully on Cara, he added, "You'll have to been seen in the cantina. Word of a beautiful woman such as you will get back to *La Serpiente*, then let's hope the bastard will take the bait."

"Where will you and Craig be?" Cara asked, taking off her watch and the silver Celtic cross she always wore.

"You won't see us, but we will be close by. Craig can track the wind across the desert in a dust storm, so know we are there. From the first contact on, you'll be constantly under watch as you're transported from one location to the next. Don't say or do anything that—well, none of us needs to be reminded that Jake is right about the dangers. One slipup could jeopardize your lives."

The sun peeked from behind the clouds, streaming through the open window and highlighting the array of autopsy pictures Jake had pinned to wall behind her desk. She couldn't bring herself go home to the ranch without Cara. Saying goodbye had almost torn her heart out, and the intuitive sixth sense that had always given her the edge in profiling was firing signals all around her.

She had been wracking her brain looking at those same pictures for almost three hours trying to find something, anything that might be a clue. Still, each time her eyes and mind would stop and concentrate on the curious welt that looked almost like a brand on the neck of one of the Jane Does. Intrusive rumblings from her stomach reminded her that she had not eaten that day, although food was the furthest thought from her mind. Still, she removed her cell phone from the charger and headed for Maria's Café.

As she walked down the street, the sounds of children playing filtered in past the honking horns and ever-present Latino rhythms emanating from almost every doorway. She wondered why the children weren't in school until it dawned on her that it was Saturday. As she continued, she stopped to watch a group of boys cracking rocks off a bench with a whip. She smiled, remembering how she and Matt and Sandro had used Maria's prize hen's eggs for their targets when they were kids and how Maria had nearly strangled all three of them—not just for destroying her eggs, but for the mess they had made on her patio.

Just as Jake reached for the door of Maria's Café, she heard the raucous laughter of the boys, three successive stinging pops of a whip, and more laughter. She paused with her hand on the door, something desperately trying to edge its way into her mind, her mind effectively refusing to let it in. She shook her head, turned her thoughts to the setting sun, and wondered where Cara was.

Chapter Twelve

Angel Torres focused his eyes keenly ahead on the long, straight band of Interstate 15 that cut through Mexico. Aside from the occasional hitchhiker, the ride had been largely uneventful. Except for the sweltering heat. Sweat rolled down his face, and he cast an apologetic shrug toward Cara, who had been noticeably quiet since they had crossed at Nogales.

"Sorry about no air. Didn't think driving up in a cushy air-conditioned car would convince anyone we were poor Mexican border runners. Besides, the bank still owns it, and getting it back stripped to the bare metal," Torres chuckled, "I don't think that would go over too good."

He owed the woman sitting next to him. Because of her dogged persistence, he had been able to reclaim his life and return to his family after being falsely accused and tried for murder. The day he first laid eyes on the intimidating attorney passed through his mind. He had been appointed a public defender at first, only to have him replaced before they had even met. His mother, seeing how her son was being shuffled around in the legal system, had contacted her friend Lara Sandoval—who worked at some high-profile law firm in Tucson—while he had nervously paced his cell for days, knowing a nonpaying Mexican was not going to be a priority for anyone. The next thing he knew, he no longer had a public defender but some big-shot lawyer who was taking his case for free.

He would never forget how she entered the stark, gunmetal grey room with a sophisticated air of both grace and authority and directed the officer—no, it had been more of a command—to take the cuffs off her client and leave the room. Then she walked over to him, leaning close to his face and focusing those brown pools of intimidation on him for what seemed like an eternity. Her eyes never wavered from his as she calmly fanned out in front of him half a dozen photographs of the woman he was accused of murdering.

"Did you in any way harm or kill this woman?" she had asked point-blank, refusing to release him from her inscrutable gaze. He never looked down at the photos; knowing he was innocent, he did not need to see them. And in that moment, he had glimpsed into the unnamable truth behind the eyes that bored into his. An unspoken trust passed between them. Inexplicably, as if by instinct, he found himself entrusting his life to this brash woman who would fight for his life and his freedom. "No, I did not kill or harm this woman," he remembered saying, almost trance-like in his honesty while his eyes never left hers. From then on, she had not abandoned him, never gave him cause to distrust her, never disappointed him.

Now, when she needed him, was relying on him to help her, he would not fail her. It was his chance to return the trust by accompanying her into the heart of Mexico and the fires of hell—where unspeakable, unspoken atrocities happened daily; where people disappeared, never again to be seen, their picked-clean, bleached bones scattered like worthless litter beneath the merciless desert sun. She was his guardian angel. Discreetly crossing himself, he silently pledged to protect her, even if it cost him his life.

The old Chevy truck was literally bathed in heat that radiated down from the sun and seemed to percolate back up from the asphalt. Sweat trickled down Cara's back, saturating the thin blouse and sticking it to her and the truck seat. She had been to Mexico many times with her grandfather when he crossed to hire pickers. There were always so many waiting for work, and the status of being a Cipriano picker preceded itself. The kindly Italian was renowned among the throngs of would-be laborers for his fair wages and respectable treatment, as well as for providing safe passage to and from his vineyard at harvest time.

The hiring was a favorite time for her, and each year brought a new enthusiastic anticipation of the trek. It was their special time, too. They would make a day of it, shopping at the local merchants for supplies to outfit the newest assemblage of Cipriano pickers. Smiling as the old truck lumbered through the endless scenic vista around her, Cara affectionately remembered her grandfather's proud grin spreading across his face while he watched her barter with the best of them. It became a traditional contest with the merchants as well, each year, eagerly welcoming the challenge and the business from the tall, gangly novice vintner.

Her smile slipped from her face as more of the past intruded. For every good there was an evil, and no joy could be savored without the mirror of sorrow. As the bond between grandfather and granddaughter had grown stronger over those wonderful years, so too had the distance, resentment, and enmity of her older brothers intensified. But this trip into Mexico was different. A shadowy prickle of foreboding permeated the air inside the cab as the old truck chugged deeper into Mexico.

Calming thoughts of Jake sidetracked her from the impossible heat and the uneasy feeling that something was amiss. Jake's love, a healing balm that soothed the anger and guilt in her soul, washed over her as she closed her eyes against the glaring sun. She watched again, her hand sliding over Jake's cool, soft skin, reliving the sensuous memory of hours that passed as seconds as their bodies and minds created their own perfect rhythm—passionate moments that had nurtured their closeness. Cara agonized even now over her decision to go against Jake's wishes by going to Mexico. Would Jake be there for her when she returned? Would it jeopardize their relationship? She'd seen the torment in her eyes, the fear and hurt on her face. *I disappointed her. I should have stayed. Please, Jake, understand and know I will be back!*

Lecherous, prying eyes from Mexicans loitering on street corners and hanging out of doorways followed Cara as she and Torres navigated down the filthy street, which reeked with the stench of garbage and urine, toward the El Cid Hotel. Ever wary, Cara observed the dark eyes and movement around them; she followed close to Torres with her hand pressed into the crook of his arm. Her hair was pulled back simply, accentuating her olive skin and noble cheekbones, into a single, loose braid that hung down the back of her white blouse. Quite aware that this could be the performance of their lives, both she and Torres feigned numerous smiles at the suggestive remarks and obscene gestures, never knowing which of the men might be one of *La Serpiente's* lookouts.

In a protective gesture, Torres closed his hand over hers as he slowed to bring her closer. He smiled encouragingly and nodded, leaning in close enough to whisper near the tiny transceiver lodged behind her ear under her hair. "Hey Matt, *amigo*, you're listening. Right?"

He put his arm around Cara's shoulders, mindful of the man at the entryway of El Cid watching them. Focusing his concentration on the mission, he led Cara into the hotel and headed for the cantina and the contact. If there were any doubts or reservations from either of them, they were put aside. There was no turning back now.

Idly toying with her food, Jake absentmindedly ate a bite as her concern for Cara grew.

"You should eat more, Jake," Maria chided gently. "Pushing yourself this way, it is not good. Matt does not listen to me either, even though his nightmares have returned since this terrible thing in the desert started."

Jake, half listening to Maria's voice in the background, vaguely remembered Matt telling her about the nightmares he had after Desert Storm when he was investigating the rape and murder of several young Kuwaiti women.

"And I bet you are not drinking enough water in this heat. It's hot enough to fry eggs on the sidewalk."

Unthinking, Jake voiced her thoughts. "I know, Maria. I thought I should eat, but I'm just not hungry. I'm so worried about Cara." Realizing Maria had stopped talking she quickly, but awkwardly added, "and Matt."

Maria stepped around the counter. Squeezing Jake's shoulder compassionately, she asked, "Why aren't you down there with them, then?"

The straightforwardness of the question jolted Jake. She looked up at Maria, but her gaze strayed beyond her to her own private demons that had pushed and controlled her emotions most of her life. Her father's voice echoed in her head. *Do right, Jake, just do right.* She loved her father, but her relentless drive to measure up to his expectations had isolated her heart from the joy of living—and the joy of love.

"The fact that it could cost all of us our jobs and possibly our lives, anger, stubbornness. Shall I continue?" Jake shook her head. Who was she trying to kid? More to herself than to Maria, she admitted, "None of that matters at all, does it? If you love, truly love, it doesn't matter. You should be together."

Maria studied Jake thoughtfully, sensing a change. She had watched Jake, an inquisitive child, grow into an awkward teenager and then into a beautiful, caring woman. She loved her as her own. Jake's words touched her heart, and Maria could no longer be a silent witness to what she knew.

"Does she know how much you love her?"

Astonished at Maria's perception, yet uncertain of what she would see, Jake hesitantly raised her face. Expecting Maria's criticism and negative judgment for loving a woman or anyone other than Matt, she was startled when only kindness and understanding reached out to her from Maria's soulful brown eyes. There was no point in pretending.

"Yes, I think she does, at least I hope she does." Jake took both of Maria's hands in hers. "I am so sorry. I never meant to hurt Matt, Maria. Please believe that."

"We cannot make people love us, Jacquelyn. I have always known Matt would not hold your heart. He just could not see beyond his love for you."

Sorrow etched over Jake's face at the words. Realizing how her words had affected Jake, Maria reassured her.

"What is important is that we do love and that we are loved in return, no matter the person. It is the soul we love, child. Be it man or woman, we must follow our hearts. I have seen the way she looks at you too, Jacquelyn. There is an enduring love behind those eyes. She is a good woman. So brave in her desire to help the less fortunate—and a people who are not even her own. This is a dangerous thing they do."

Jake scolded herself for doing nothing when she knew without doubt she should have gone, should have been there for Cara, for them all. "Oh, Maria! Why do I have to be so stubborn? Why didn't I go with them? I'm a trained FBI agent. She's a lawyer, for God's sake."

Cupping Jake's face in her hands, Maria reminded her, "There is nothing stopping you now. Do you know where they are?"

"Yes," Jake said as she quickly flipped open her phone and speed-dialed Matt's cell. After a few seconds, she closed her phone, worry evident on her face. All she had gotten was a message that the customer was out of service range. The resurgence of that old signal, a premonition of something not being right—the same one she had the day her father was murdered—distressed her, encasing her with a sense of urgency. Her throat suddenly went dry.

"I need to go to her."

Maria gathered Jake into her arms as she often had when Jake was a child after her mother passed. "Please be safe, Jacquelyn." After one last hug, she pointed Jake toward the door. "Go to her. And tell that son of mine that he better bring you all back in one piece."

Jake ran out of the café, trying to reach Matt once more. "Matt's still not getting a signal, and Cara didn't take hers," she said aloud in exasperation. Racing her SUV around the curves of downtown Nogales, Jake headed for the border crossing.

"*Mañana, por favor,*" repeated the bartender at the El Cid. "*Los Gatos mañana, sí?*"

"*Sí, señor,*" answered Torres over his shoulder as he returned to where Cara stood by the doorway fending off a group of ogling men.

"Well?" questioned Cara as she turned and ignored the advances.

"He said come back tomorrow. Now let's get out of here, too many eyes watching us."

Torres and Cara made their way down the litter-strewn street, quickly turning the first corner to get out of sight before they attempted any contact with Matt.

"Matt, are you there, did you hear?" Cara spoke in a low tone.

"Copy that. We're with you. Go back to the hotel where you have rooms. It's a waiting game now. They'll want to see how much money they can squeeze out of you.

Tomorrow they'll ask for more. If you don't have it, they'll offer alternatives for the passage."

Cara's voice turned menacing. "Are we talking about certain favors as the alternative, Matt?"

He was silent for a moment. Worriedly pinching the bridge of his nose, he had to be honest with her. "That usually is the case when a girl—or a beautiful woman such as you—is involved, and her family is desperate to get across. Don't worry about it, we're closer than you know. Go to the hotel and try to get some sleep. It's not the Comfort Suites. Hell, it's not even in Motel 6 territory, but Torres was able to get two rooms next to each other. To be on the safe side, brace a chair against the door and don't open it to anyone."

Cara lay awake listening to the Latino music from the cantina downstairs. She had tossed and turned, unable to sleep thinking about Jake and the hurt she had seen in her hazel eyes. *Oh, Jake, I wanted to stay with you, I did. Please understand I have to try to help stop this.* Restless, she slid out of the lumpy bed and went to stare out the window. The little town effervesced with activity as if it were the middle of the day—mostly drunks shouting and backfiring cars racing up and down the street below.

Cara thought she heard a light tapping on her door. Stepping noiselessly back to the bed, she reached under the pillow for the pistol Torres had slipped to her when they had reached the hotel. Another faint tap sent her quietly to stand next to the door. At the sound of the doorknob creaking, she chambered a round into the 9mm as quietly as she could before easing the chair away. She held her breath and waited. As the door began to open, she grasped the knob, flung the door solidly back, and quickly straddled a figure as it fell. Even before they hit the floor, Cara was pressing the pistol barrel into a forehead. Just as her finger closed on the trigger, the blinking neon light from the hotel sign illuminated the face of the intruder.

"Jesus Christ! Jake! What are you doing here? My god, I could have killed you!" Cara began to shake uncontrollably as she used both hands to lower the gun to the floor. "Damn!" Her heart was beating so hard her chest hurt, and she couldn't slow her breathing. Jake slid her arms around Cara's waist, holding her tightly. "If anything ever happened to you I—"

Jake silenced her with a passionate kiss, then softly whispered into Cara's ear, "You talk too much, Counselor."

A knock on the door followed by Torres's voice asking her if she was up propelled Cara into the glaring light of morning. She pulled the worn bedspread over Jake's naked body. "Still sleeping even in all this noise," she chuckled while grabbing the sheet off the floor. Wrapping it around her own naked body, she went to the door and opened it a crack.

"Uh, I," she cleared the huskiness from her voice, "can you give me a few minutes? I'll meet you in your room in half an hour."

Torres blushed as he delivered his message. "Cara, Matt wants us to meet him now, just outside of town. I know the place. He's got some new information."

"Ok. I'll see you in a bit." She started to close the door, but Torres's voice stopped her.

"Craig was watching the hotel to make sure you were safe last night. He saw Jake, followed her, and watched her come up here. Matt's real worried, Cara. Somebody else might have seen her, too." He lowered his eyes. "I'm sorry, my friend. I will give you both some time."

Jake watched Cara lean against the closed door, then let her eyes travel down her lover's perfect body as the sheet slipped down her bare back to reveal exquisite hips. They had made love throughout the night, and she felt her arousal building, wanting her again.

"Well, I guess the proverbial cat is out of the bag. Is this all right with you, my love?" Cara asked, concerned, dropping the sheet as she neared the bed. She allowed Jake to pull her back into bed.

In a smoky voice that left no doubt as to her intentions, Jake ordered, "Come back to bed, Counselor, and we can discuss it."

All that remained was the sensation of Jake nibbling across her chin and down her neck, each touch intermingled with the whispered words that governed her heart: "I love you, Cara."

Jake left the hotel first, after coffee and sweet breads in Torres's room. She didn't want to blow their cover and jeopardize the operation, so she planned on going to La Cebolla, about twenty-five miles away, where Sandro had a ranch. It had been a long time since she had taken the time to visit. The ranch was close enough if they needed her, and no one would ask questions.

When she arrived, there wasn't a sign of anyone. Once more, she took in the beauty of the place, but still she always wondered why Sandro chose to build on the Mexican side of the border when he had been deeded several acres at the vineyards in Sonoita by Matt's father when they were children. Sandro would always smile in that charming, boyish way and say he could get much more for his hard-earned dollars in Mexico. She walked around the house to the corral looking for any sign of life, but again found no one. She hooked her boot in the railing of the corral and boosted herself up to admire a beautiful Appaloosa who had wandered over to check her out. Her eyes roamed over the magnificent spotted horse to the striped hooves.

At that moment, Jake's mind chose to unleash the cloaked images that had hovered just beneath the surface. There in front of her, clearly delineated in the dried, caked-up dirt around the watering trough, was the indentation of a marked boot heel—an exact replica of the boot print she'd been staring at for weeks. In her mind, the images and sounds clicked off like slides in a projector. She heard the snap of a whip, Sandro's laughter, his eyes floating out of the boot print. It all came together.

No, it can't be. Oh my god, it can't be! The air and all around her stood still; she forgot how to breathe. She stepped blindly off the railing reaching out to grab a post before her knees buckled under her. The next thing she knew she was on her hands and knees, retching.

Torres and Cara drove to the outskirts of Santa Ana for the meet with Matt and Craig. She wasn't sure what Matt knew about Jake's visit the previous night or if he suspected they were lovers. It made her uncomfortable keeping it from him; he deserved to know. But now wasn't the time or place. Matt was brewing coffee on an open campfire when she and Torres arrived. Standing slowly, he offered them both a cup.

"We have a tip on two possible locations of *coyote* activity. I think we should check it out this morning, and I don't want you two in town alone."

Matt began to break camp. He hadn't said anything about Jake, but Cara could feel the tension between them. *Well, no point in avoiding this.* She walked over to where Matt was pouring the last of the coffee over the fire, making sure it was out.

"Matt, we need to talk." He raised his head to look at Cara. "About Jake." Cara looked him straight in the eyes. "And me."

The pain and hurt on his face was evident; he looked down and poked at the smoldering campfire a moment, then looked back to Cara.

"I won't pretend to understand the relationship between two women. Hell, figuring out the one between a man and woman is hard enough. I can't tell you this didn't kick me in the heart. This I can tell you, though. I love her, always have, and I know she doesn't love easy. If you don't take care of her, or if you break her heart, you'll answer to me. Now one question, then we need to get moving. Do you love her?"

Without hesitation, Cara answered him, never losing eye contact. "Yes, I do, Matt, more than I ever thought possible."

He studied her face, then nodded and tossed her the sleeping bags. "We better get a move on, they can move the illegals to another location if they get suspicious. If we can pick up one of the lead *coyotes*, we might have a shot at their boss."

As Cara watched Matt walk away to load up his gear, she couldn't help but think how much he loved Jake and what a loyal friend he was.

Matt and Craig stopped on the dirt road where it split in two. Matt got out and went back to the old Chevy pickup Torres was driving.

"Craig and I will take the fork to the right and you two can check out the other one. Don't do anything heroic, use your two-way radios and stand back until we get there if you find anything before we do."

For some reason, Cara felt edgy as they maneuvered down the deserted road. Even in the oppressive heat, the skin on her arms prickled up with goose bumps while a tingly, gnawing sensation crept through her stomach. She couldn't explain it, but she knew it was connected to Jake. *What is it, Jake? What's wrong?* With every mile that snaked by, the feeling got stronger.

Torres was jumpy, too. A covey of Gambel's quail flushed and flew in front of them, causing him to swerve sharply to the right and off the edge of the road. After that, Cara noticed that every few seconds he was wiping his sweaty face across his shirt sleeve.

Then, trying to downplay his nervousness, he started talking. "My country is beautiful, so untouched in many ways. The simply majesty is to me such a contrast to how many of my people have to live, exist really. I often dream of how great a country Mexico could have been and still could be if not for our history of corrupt leadership. Historically, my people have worked hard with very little to show for their labor. Always, we have dreams and hopes of a better life for our children, as our parents did. A life without hunger and to live without fear, that's all they ask. Things are getting better, slowly, but we have a long way to go."

Cara looked a long time at the proud Mexican. He had fled his country and sought asylum in America, yet here he was risking his life coming back to help stop the senseless killing of Mexico's young women. "I admire you and your people's struggle to make this country a place not to leave, but to stay and try to have a good life. Thank you for helping us."

"No. It is for me to thank you, my friend, and your country for allowing me to come there. I love Mexico and my people, it is where my heart is. But," he shrugged, "I am one man. I had to provide for my family."

Abruptly, Torres pulled over as he rounded a curve in the bumpy dirt road that was little more than a trail winding through the scrubby brush. Just ahead was a clearing where a barn and several ramshackle buildings dotted the landscape.

"What do you think, Cara? It looks abandoned. I don't see anyone around."

"I don't either. Why don't we check it out first before we radio Matt and Craig?"

"Sounds like a plan. Let me pull the truck over in those bushes so it's not sitting in plain sight."

After stowing the truck, they walked back up to the road and headed for the clearing ahead.

"You check that one," she said, pointing to a dilapidated barn several yards away from two other buildings. "I'll check out those two. Do you have your radio?"

Torres patted his shirt pocket. "Yes, I will call and you me, if you find anything." He reached out to touch Cara's shoulder lightly. "Be careful, my friend, the serenity can be deceiving."

As Cara approached the boarded-up shack next to the barn, she thought she could hear a muffled noise, like a moan. Easing around to the backside of the building, she peeked through a crack only to be greeted by a sight that turned her stomach. She managed to pry a board loose and was able to see that there were probably fifty people jammed into a space no bigger than most people's bathrooms. The outside temperature had to be over a hundred degrees; she could only imagine how intense the heat was inside the shed. A young boy, black eyes dominating his entire face, stared back at her. She motioned for him to come closer, then told him she was there to help, that she would get them out. But the boy stopped her, saying he was afraid for his family. If they were caught, *La Serpiente* would kill them all. As Cara was about to stand, she heard the crack of a whip and almost simultaneously felt the stinging leather wrap around her neck. She was dragged backwards across the hot, dusty ground when suddenly something, a heavy boot she thought, connected with her head. A sudden burst of pain shot through her as she slipped into darkness.

What seemed like hours later, Cara's eyes opened to a grungy ceiling bathed in the light of a single incandescent bulb. The bed on which she lay was hard, nothing more than straw stuffed into burlap. Her neck hurt; she wanted to reach up to feel the deep furrow where the whip had cut into her flesh, but as she struggled to move, she realized her hands and feet were tied. The door in front of her opened, and a chilling voice penetrated the shadows.

"Ah, good. I see you're awake. I have missed your company."

Cara tried to focus her eyes on the figure standing partially masked by the deep shadows. "Where is my brother? Who are you?"

"Who I am is of no concern to you." His blood-curdling laugh caused her skin to crawl. "You won't be around long enough to fully appreciate that knowledge, so you can stop your little charade, Cara Vittore. Yes, I know who you are and what you are doing here. And as for Angel," he gestured over his shoulder to where a bleeding Torres hung stretched between two posts, "well, let's just say that when I am finished with him, the little *pendejo* will be praying to be with his namesakes."

The trademark whip of *La Serpiente* uncoiled behind him as he situated himself several feet behind the bare-backed Torres. With lightening speed and deadly accuracy, the whip spanned the distance in a split second, slicing deeply into Torres's flesh. Blood flowed freely from the first lashing. One arch of leather after another cut deep grooves into Torres, who had yet to cry out from the certain agony he was in. Blood poured down his back, mixing with his sweat.

The whip master never once spoke. He merely chuckled, then laughed with apparent pleasure with each strike. The man was truly deriving pleasure from his actions. After several minutes, Torres's legs buckled, causing his head to loll forward. His limp body sagged to the dirt as far as the restraints allowed him. Thankfully, he had passed out after the fourth lash, no longer feeling the slicing devil's whip.

Cara's anger exploded as she struggled against her restraints. "You bastard! I hope you burn in hell!"

He recoiled the whip slowly, almost sensuously playing his hands across the leather. The handsome face twisted into a sardonic smile followed by a low chuckle. "Not today, *chica*, not today."

Cara felt the bile rising in her throat as he approached her with something that looked like a cattle prod. She braced herself for the inevitable pain. After the third shock, everything went black. All she could remember before she passed out was the malicious man's voice taunting her, telling her he was softening her up to be more receptive, but that he didn't want to take all the fight out of her.

She didn't know how long she had been out when she regained consciousness, but she guessed it couldn't have been too long. The methodical torture with the cattle prod that had sent sadistic electrical charges throughout her body left her bruised and aching. The blood on her lip where she had bitten down against the pain was still fresh, and her lip was still bleeding. She tried to call to Torres, who was an unrecognizable bloody pulp, hanging grotesque and lifeless. Her mouth was so dry she couldn't form the words. The light was too bright and the room spun. But as she looked around the dingy enclosure desperately thinking of a way to free herself, her eyes stopped when she saw that they were not alone. There by the window was a guard. Her movement had drawn his attention, and now he walked over and stood looking down at her.

"*Sí, La Serpiente* always picks the prettiest of the bunch to play with."

A grimy hand pawed at her body, roughly twisting one of her nipples, while the other hand groped at his groin.

"I would not mind a piece of you myself, *puta*." He leered obscenely, "Perhaps when he is done with you, he will give to me what is left."

He returned to his post at the window. Cara felt as if she were going to be sick, but she fought to keep it down. Her mind, still lucid despite the excruciating pain she had suffered, was taunted by an elusive thought that just wouldn't come clear. She frantically struggled at the ropes that tied her hands above her head. Then the thought came.

He's a true sadist, and he's enjoying the torture. This is just the buildup for him, it's what he needs. After he's done, he will kill me and Torres, if he isn't dead already.

The grungy man at the window flashed a lewd grin at her. She excited him, and he felt himself grow hard watching her fruitless struggle to get free.

"You are working too hard, *puta*. You should save your energy until *La Serpiente* gets back. It will be a long day and night for you." The smile on his face turned lustful as he approached Cara and released the rope that tied her legs. "Fortunately, the boss had to attend to a small matter and won't be back for awhile."

He pulled out his penis, jerked down her jeans and lay down on top of her. She struggled to throw his filthy body off her. She could smell his foul breath and body odor as he entered her. *Oh God! Please, don't let this happen!* At that moment, Cara was able to detach herself emotionally, returning in her mind to the part she had to play, no longer aware of the grunting body above her.

Jake felt strong hands under her arms pulling her up and heard a voice telling her to hurry.

"Come, you must get up. You need to go. He will be back soon."

Jake gulped air as she tried to regain her equilibrium. "Are you talking about *Señor* Sandro?"

The young Hispanic woman was clearly frightened, constantly casting furtive glances over her shoulder like a doe surveying her surroundings for threats. "I do not know this *Señor* Sandro you speak of, *señorita*."

Dizzy, Jake leaned against a corral post to steady herself. "The man you're afraid of, what is his name?"

"We only know him by *La Serpiente*. Hurry, you must go!"

"What are you doing here, how do you know this man? Why is he here at Sandro's ranch?"

"I have told you, *señorita*, I know no one called Sandro. There is only *La Serpiente* with the stinging whip, like a snake's tongue it is. His men took our money and promised to get my father and me across to the United States. Then they wanted more, and we did not have it. My father was taken, and I," her face lowered in shame, "I was brought here to this place." Her hand went up to cover the marks on her throat.

Sickening images of the mutilated girls rushed across Jake's mind. *What does a cold-blooded serial killer look like? How do you recognize an abomination that can torture, rape, and then mutilate another human being? A faceless chameleon, always managing to stay one step ahead of us...hiding in plain sight as a trusted friend.* She felt the blood in her veins run cold as she asked, "Please, can you describe this *La Serpiente*?"

"He is tall, *señorita*, with the eyes of *El Diablo* himself. When he strikes with his whip, the eyes come alive with evil."

An inner voice, as she already thought the unthinkable, taunted Jake to ask one last question. "Is he missing the tip of his right little finger?"

"*Sí, señorita*, he is marked so by *El Diablo*."

Jake leaned against the post for support, her head spinning and knees threatening to give way again. "Oh my god. I have to get to Cara and Matt. I have to warn them."

"You must leave. Quickly. He will kill you, and me for helping you, *señorita*."

Jake righted herself and looked out toward the mountains, trying to figure out how to get in touch with Matt since the cell phone was not an option. Then, as she unseeingly gazed at the abstract pattern of spots on the Appaloosa, her mind in shock, she heard the crunch of boots behind her. When she turned, she was face to face with Sandro, who was glaring at the girl. He had a hard grip on her arm as he closed the distance to Jake. An awkward silence pervaded the corral.

"Well, Jake, my love, what brings you down?"

"It's been a while since I've spent time at the hacienda, and I needed a day away."

She tried to keep the tone of her voice level, not wanting to betray her newfound knowledge about the man she had for so long called friend. But Sandro was appraising her every word and move. She shuffled a foot in the dust; his eyes darted to it and then back to her eyes. She tried to avoid meeting his eyes; he took notice. Stepping toward her, he clasped her hand into his.

"My dearest Jake, be my guest," he said with a sweeping gesture toward his sprawling adobe home. Jake shook off his grip and headed for the house. She was a good ten paces ahead when she heard the whip snap. She wheeled around in time to see the girl clawing at the leather that was binding her throat. Sandro quickly closed the space between them, dragging the girl behind.

"Now you will not run again, will you, *chica*?" He hit her across the face, splitting her lip. "Now go back inside and do as you were told!"

Hurriedly, he snagged Jake by the arm. "Not so fast, my love," he drawled, then pushed her toward the house. Jake tried to jerk free of Sandro's grip, infuriating him. "I said, be my guest, Jake! And I meant now!" he boomed, stilling her breath with a voice that was almost unrecognizable as he forced her up the stone steps and inside the house.

Turning her head toward a noise to her left, Cara saw the same boy she had seen in the shed earlier. He squeezed through the loose boards, crawled against the wall in the darkness, small and unseen, moving silently toward her. Cara's eyes darted back and forth between him and the man who had raped her, who stood across the room smoking.

The boy slowly sneaked beside Cara and untied the ropes around her hands. She pulled her torn shirt across her bruised and bitten breasts then shushed him with a finger to his lips, motioning with her eyes to the window where they could see the guard's back. When she pushed him, the boy understood that she meant for him to go back out. After he disappeared back through the boards, with as little movement as possible she pulled her jeans up over her aching hips and rolled silently off the cot.

Picking up an old two by four, she crept silently up behind the guard. With rage in her heart, she brought the board down on his head. He crumpled to his knees. Still she hit him, again and again, only stopping when he fell into the dirt floor unconscious, his head gashed and bloody. She moved one step backwards, dropping the board. Pushing the images of what had happened to her and what she had just done to the guard out of her mind, she grabbed his gun and the knife from his belt and ran over to Torres, who still hung limply from his restraints. She cut him down and gently eased him to the ground, searching for a pulse. It was weak and thready, but he was alive.

She ran out to the shed where the captive Mexicans were being held and she released them, pointing to a water tank and hose. She grabbed a bucket, filled it with water, and ran back to Torres. Cupping the water in her hands, she wet his face and lips. After a moment, he started to come around and was able to swallow on his own. Though his voice was raw, he whispered, "Cara..."

"Shh. It's okay, Torres. The guard is down, and *La Serpiente* is nowhere to be seen. I've released the people in the shed. Matt hasn't heard from us in hours, and if he and Craig are alive they'll be looking for us. Jake was going to Sandro's ranch. Do you know how I can get there from here? I've got to get to Jake and contact Matt if it's not too late."

He was gritting his teeth as each breath assaulted him with agonizing pain. "Cara, *La Serpiente* is Sandro! I Recognized him from when I crossed at Sasabe. Even without his uniform, I recognized him. Matt...Craig...can't be far...west...go back to the fork in the road," he coughed out in a raspy mumble as his head slumped over.

Cara's mind couldn't process what she was hearing. Her face paled and her heart heaved into her throat when the implication came clear. "But if—oh God, no! Jake—Jake was going to Sandro's ranch in La Cebolla when she left this morning!"

"Transceiver?" Torres whispered.

"No, it's gone, lost. The dead signal should already have alerted them that something's happened. They can't be far off."

"Go, I'll be fine." He clenched his jaw against the pain. "Matt stashed a backup two-way behind the seat of the truck. Try to get Matt or the Border Patrol. They can relay a message to him."

Cara raced out to where dozens of grateful immigrants were still quenching their thirst. As she neared them, they all mumbled and murmured their heartfelt thanks for her help. Amid the noise, she managed to get their attention.

"Do any of you know this area? Where we are? Or how to get to a main road that will get me back to La Cebolla and Sandro de Zavala's ranch?"

A leathery-skinned elderly man raised his eyes to Cara as he stepped forward slowly, putting his fear aside. "*Sí, señorita*, this road behind us leads to a fork. Go to the right to get to La Cebolla. On that road, you cannot miss the turn to the hacienda."

"*Gracias, señor, gracias.* I need you to take care of my friend until I get back with help. Can you do that?" Cara questioned.

Several nodded their heads affirmatively and went inside the shed to tend to Torres.

"*Señorita.*" The old man stopped Cara. "I know this man, as I see you do, too. Be careful."

"*Gracias.*"

And with that she raced back to where they had stashed the truck. Feeling behind the seat, she located the hidden two-way. She grabbed it, leapt in the truck, and called Matt. Gunning the engine, she spun away and down the road toward La Cebolla. Her harried voice broke across the air into Matt's ear.

"Matt! Are you there? Craig, Matt, anybody!"

"We copy, Cara. What's wrong?"

"Jake. Gotta get to Jake at Sandro's ranch," she screamed into the radio.

"Is she hurt? What's going on?"

"Just listen. It's Sandro. Sandro is *La Serpiente*! Jake is at his ranch. He knows we are on to him, Matt! Can you get to her? How close are you? I'm on my way, but you may be closer!"

Matt's stomach lurched at the news. He turned the truck around, heading for Sandro's hacienda as he spoke. "We're not far, just a few minutes out."

"Torres is hurt bad. Lots of other people there needing medical attention."

"Are you okay?"

"I'm good. Just get to Jake!"

Matt and Cara both threw their radios down, driving furiously to get to the hacienda before—neither one could finish the thought.

Running the cool, hard leather whip handle down the side of her face, Sandro spoke unequivocally. "Jake, my love, you have put me in a most awkward position."

She struggled to remain calm, knowing it could be her only chance. "How could you, Sandro? Maria loves you as her son. Matt loves you as a brother. This will kill them. Why? Why kill Alejandro? My god, you're responsible for the deaths of all those innocent girls!"

He turned his back to her, ignoring her last statement. "There are far greater stakes in this little game than you could possibly know."

"I know it has to be more than just the illegal alien trade. My guess, you're smuggling drugs."

He laughed and looked back at her. "You have no idea, Jake."

Her only chance was to separate her lifelong friend from the killer he had become and pray to God it would work long enough to stall him. She could see him hesitate, so she continued to talk.

"I understand the lure of money. But the girls, Sandro. How could you be two people? How could you have done such horrible things to those girls, then sit across the table eating and laughing with Matt and Maria and me?"

Jake knew if she kept him talking, if she could put positive images in his mind, she stood a better chance of getting out alive. She knew he could kill her. But would he?

"I care about you, Sandro. I have loved you as a brother since we—you, me, Matt—could even sit a horse. We can help you, Sandro. Please let us."

"It's all a joke, you know. The idea that I always got the girls and Matt went home alone. Oh, I got them all right."

For a moment, before he paused briefly to look out the window and light a cigar, Jake glimpsed a sadness in his eyes.

"You weren't supposed to find anything. But just like your dad, you did." His voice, now tinged with a cold detachment, frightened Jake. "Like father, like daughter. Why couldn't he just stay in retirement and grow the grapes? And you. Always just too good at what you do. Right, Jake? It wouldn't have been too much longer before you connected all the dots just like your dad did. And then you had to bring that bitch Vittore down here and let her start nosing around. Lot of good it will do her where she is."

Jake's mind was a flurry of thoughts. *What does Sandro have to do with Dad? What is he talking about?* Then the cold reality hit her. *He has Cara! God, please help me.*

"Where is she?" Jake asked, keeping her emotions in check, not wanting to give Sandro any ammunition by letting him know she cared for Cara or that his mention of her dad had upset her. He was slow to answer, pacing the floor and continuously coiling and flicking and recoiling his whip.

"Please, Sandy, at least tell me if she's alive."

"She's alive. For now. More than what we can say for your meddling father."

Suddenly what Sandro was saying finally clutched her throat. Seething green eyes narrowed in rage, Jake spat, "You! You killed my father!"

A pounding on the door followed by the intrusion of one of Sandro's men prevented Jake from reacting.

"What!" yelled Sandro.

"Forgive me, *jefe*. The lookout at the crossroads, he radioed that a truck is headed this way. It's is the BP Matt Peyson and the Shadow Wolf."

For the first time, Jake saw concern on Sandro's face.

"Get the helicopter ready. Go!" Sandro grabbed Jake by the arm and jerked her toward the door. "Looks like we're going for a ride."

"Damnit, Sandro, leave me here. You don't need me. They already know it's you if they're headed here."

"Remember the rule, Jake. Utilize your resources. And you are my resource to safety."

With that, he roughly shoved her out the door toward the clearing where the chopper was warming up. In the distance, Sandro saw the telltale sign of dust belching up from the desert floor. Matt was close.

Sandro had no sooner reached the helicopter when the first shot rang out. Just as he seized the handle and yanked open the door, hoisting Jake inside, another shot rang out.

Sandro pulled his gun and fired at Matt's truck, deliberately aiming high.

Grabbing his rifle, Craig leapt from the still-moving vehicle and rolled to a shooting stance. Matt slammed to a sideways stop and leaped out, ducking behind the front end, and slammed two shots at Sandro's feet. Dust kicked up, obscuring their vision momentarily.

Taking advantage of the cover, Sandro turned to push Jake further inside the chopper. Craig, aiming from a different vantage than Matt, fired a 30-30 round, piercing Sandro's thigh. Jake, ever aware of what was happening, kicked out and landed a booted foot to the wound in his leg, knocking him back just long enough for her to jump and hit the ground running.

Seeing his insurance running off, Sandro leveled his gun on Jake's back. She was dead in his sights when suddenly he pulled back and leapt into the chopper, spiraling up and south immediately.

Cara had seen the dust cloud to the west as she raced down the dirt road. As she fishtailed into the clearing, she saw Matt. Craig was running, firing his rifle at a helicopter that was veering southward, but in seconds his target was gone. Cara searched frantically for Jake, her heart hammering against her chest. And then she saw her—sitting on her heels leaned back against Matt's truck. Not even bothering to turn the engine off, Cara sprinted from the truck toward Jake. Her chest heaved as much from fear as from exerting her tortured body, and her face had turned a pale white. She kneeled down beside her, only to have Jake fall into her arms.

"Jake, I was so scared," she whispered, her voice tremulous with fear and emotion while she stroked her left eyebrow with her thumb, then gently caressed her cheek.

Jake threw her arms around Cara, holding her tightly. "I'm okay. Are you? Did he hurt you?" Looking at Cara's torn clothes, fear gripped her. "Please tell me did—did he...?"

Cara couldn't tell her about the rape, it wasn't important now. All that mattered was that Jake was safe.

"Banged up a little, Torres got the worst of it. I just thank God I was able to get a message through to Matt and Craig."

Looking into Cara's distraught eyes, Jake saw the tears. She kissed her gently on the lips, then again, more deeply. She broke the kiss. "I love you, Counselor. We've had enough excitement to last us a lifetime." Taking Cara's hand, she sighed, "Let's go home."

Focused only on each other, neither was mindful of Craig, standing next to the truck, who ducked his head sheepishly, pretending to be interested in his boots. Nor were they conscious of Matt, who watched the scene intently, shrewdly aware that he was seeing two people who were very much in love. Dust plumed up all around him as his heart suffered doubly. It broke undeniably at the sight of Jake and Cara, so obviously in love—Cara sharing the love he had wanted with Jake. Yet a burden even harder to endure was Sandro. Desolate thoughts tore into his heart, challenging all he thought he had known.

He slowly turned his head toward the end of the clearing where Jake and Cara had walked. Then with calm precision, Matt Peyson deliberately moved his head back to the painted sky where Sandro's helicopter had disappeared. A quiet, unrelenting rage caught fire inside, rising within his throat and escalating to a silent fury. He spoke aloud through the dust-choked emptiness.

"It doesn't end here, Sandro."

New Releases From
StarCrossed Productions

Tomorrow's Promise
Radclyffe

Adrienne Pierce, buffeted by fate and abandoned by love, seeks refuge from her past as well as her uncertain future on Whitley Point, a secluded island off the coast of Maine. Tanner Whitley—young, wild, restless—and heir to a dynasty, desperately tries to escape both her destiny and the memories of a tragic loss with casual sex and wild nights, a dangerous course that may ultimately destroy her. One timeless summer, these two very different women discover the power of passion to heal—and the promise of hope that only love can bestow.

Storm Surge
KatLyn

FBI Special Agent Alex Montgomery would have given her life in the line of duty, but she lost something far more precious when she became the target of ruthless drug traffickers. Recalled to Jacksonville to aid the local authorities in infiltrating the same deadly drug ring, she has a secret agenda—revenge. Despite her unexpected involvement with Conner Harris, a tough, streetwise detective who has dedicated her life to her job at the cost of her own personal happiness, Alex vows to let nothing—and no one—stand in the way of exacting vengeance on those who took from her everything that mattered.

In the all new, revised edition of Storm Surge, these two driven women discover that even in the midst of danger, murder, and betrayal, there is one force even more powerful than duty and retribution—the connection forged by the human heart. Follow Alex and Connor in this thrilling action tale as they seek justice and the promise of a future where love might one day be found.

Beyond The Breakwater
Radclyffe

In *Beyond the Breakwater*, the sequel to *Safe Harbor*, Sheriff Reese Conlon and Doctor Tory King face the challenges of personal change as they define their lives and future together. Tory's pregnancy forces her to examine her personal needs and goals while Reese struggles with her escalating anxieties over conditions she cannot control. Twenty year-old Brianna Parker makes a sacrifice for love that threatens not just her happiness, but her life, when she returns home as the newest member of the Sheriff's department. A life-threatening accident, a suspicious fire, and the appearance of more than one woman vying for Bri's attentions makes one Provincetown summer a time of transformation as each woman learns the true meaning of love, friendship, and family.

Graceful Waters
Verda Foster & B L Miller

Joanna Carey, senior instructor at Sapling Hill, wasn't looking for anything more than completing one more year at the facility and getting that much closer to her private dream, a small cabin on a quiet lake. She was tough and smart, and she had a plan for her life.

When tough Instructor Carey meets angry and disillusioned Grace Waters, neither is prepared for what comes next. Stubborn and angry Grace meets her match in Carey, the strong and disciplined woman who's determined to help Grace help herself. What she's not expecting is that Grace will break through her own defenses. Together they will change each other's lives in ways that neither thought possible.

Visit us at www.StarCrossedProductions.com